# Treetop

Dr Lively —

I admire you for standing up to the Radical homosexuals for so many years!

# Treetop

By J. J. Dyer

XULON ELITE

Xulon Press Elite
555 Winderley Pl, Suite 225
Maitland, FL 32751
407.339.4217
www.xulonpress.com

Unless otherwise indicated, Scripture quotations taken from the Holy Bible,
New International Version (NIV). Copyright © 1990 by The B. B. Kirkbride
Bible Company, Inc. Used by permission. All rights reserved.

Paperback ISBN-13: 979-8-86851-725-9
Hard Cover ISBN-13: 979-8-86851-726-6
Ebook ISBN-13: 979-8-86851-727-3

# Dedication

Guardian Angels are possibly the most unacknowledged sentinels in existence. I wonder how many times their unseen interventions have protected us from our own foolishness. I am grateful God has entrusted them to keep a hedge of protection around us as we stumble along on our paths of sanctification. In *Treetop*, Rebekah's and Jonas' guardian angels had to be working overtime, yet they are not mentioned once in the story—unknowledged, again. This book is dedicated to their watchful presence.

*They are watching*
*Psalm 91:11*

# A Note on Treetop

*T*reetop is an imaginative tale related to a historical event in the Bible—a historical event about which God reveals few details. Being careful to remain faithful to what details are revealed in Scripture, I created the Treetop world where this story unfolds. As long as fantasy stories do not contradict God's revealed Word, they can be entertaining and thought-provoking in a good way. I hope you find *Treetop* that kind of story.

# Table of Contents

# Illustrations

**Map of Treetop**

**Coulter Pines**

# Chapter 1:

# Sit-rock

It was a very cold Christmas Eve morning when Rebekah and Jonas went outside to play. Their mom had said they could go to the sit-rock before breakfast and drink some hot cocoa. Rebekah grabbed the thermos of cocoa Mom had made for them as they walked out the door. When the cold air hit their faces, Jonas began to have second thoughts about going outside.

"It's so cozy in the house and it's freezing out here. Why don't we just drink the hot cocoa by the Christmas tree?" asked Jonas.

Rebekah zipped up her jacket and started putting on her mittens.

"It's more fun to drink hot cocoa in the cold," replied Rebekah. "We can go up on our favorite sit-rock and watch Mama and Sarah make breakfast in the kitchen. I opened the shutters so we could see the kitchen and the Christmas tree. We can pretend we're lost and freezing in a thick, scary forest and trying to find our way home. Come on, Jonas!"

Jonas nodded in agreement as they both crossed the grass toward the rock steps leading to the brush.

"Let's pretend wolves are chasing us and we'll only be safe on our rock," suggested Jonas.

Rebekah and Jonas looked at each other, smiled, and began racing up the hill toward the sit-rock—giggling and looking back as their imaginations made them feel like they really were running from wolves.

Out of breath, but sitting safely on the rock, Rebekah opened the thermos and filled the large cap with steaming cocoa.

"They can't get us up here!" Jonas said confidently.

Rebekah looked over the edge of the rock and wasn't too sure about that. She passed the cup to Jonas so he could take a sip of cocoa.

They passed the cup of cocoa back and forth between them as they talked. They watched Mom and Sarah in the kitchen, and they saw their brothers, John and Daniel, in the living room reading by the Christmas tree. It was a cozy sight, and Rebekah was glad she remembered to open the shutters before going outside.

Jonas noticed that the clouds were getting bigger and darker as the wind picked up a bit. He laid on his back and began watching the dark clouds pass by overhead.

"Rebekah, look at that cloud up there! It looks like a wolf." Jonas was pointing to a huge cloud directly over their rock.

Rebekah laid back and began watching the clouds, too. With warm tummies full of hot cocoa and with their jacket hoods pulled over their heads to keep warm, they were having fun finding all kinds of shapes in the clouds above them. It was a wonderful start to their Christmas Eve.

After playing their cloud game for a while, it seemed like it had gotten colder.

"I'm freezing," shivered Rebekah. "I'll be right back. I am going to ask Mom for more hot cocoa."

Rebekah grabbed the thermos and climbed down the rock. Jonas watched her disappear down the dirt path. He then turned his head back skyward to watch the clouds again. The biggest, blackest cloud he'd seen all morning passed overhead and made everything seem darker and colder. The cloud looked just like a big old Grizzly bear.

Rebekah wasn't gone for more than a few minutes when Jonas heard her running back up the path shouting his name.

"Jonas! Jonas!"

Jonas sat up and saw her red hair bobbing above the top of the brush as she ran up the lower path. Her hood was off her head and her hair was being blown back by her running and the cold wind. Jonas was wondering how the cold wind had appeared so fast when Rebekah cried out again, "Jonas, they're coming! They're coming up the drive!"

"Who's coming up the drive?" Jonas asked, looking toward the driveway.

"Wolves!" Rebekah screamed, "Five of them coming this way!"

Jonas couldn't see any wolves because he couldn't see any driveway. All he could see was a thick wall of fog that must have blown in on the wind from the lower valley while he was watching the clouds. The fog gobbled up the water tank and the tool shed as it headed up the hill. It was right behind Rebekah!

Rebekah reached the sit-rock out of breath with a frightened look on her face.

"We've got to get to the rock fort. This rock is not high enough to keep us safe. If they try to get us, we're better protected in the fort!"

Jonas was squinting into the fog in the direction of the drive when they both heard something moving in the brush a little ways down the path. Rebekah bolted for the rock fort. Jonas climbed down the rock and raced after Rebekah just as an eerie howl pierced the fog.

Rebekah first reached what was supposed to be their rock fort. Instead of their three-sided rock fort, she found a jumble of huge boulders leaning against and on top of one another. Jonas came up beside her and stared at the rock pile in disbelief. Their rock fort with the tree growing through it was gone!

They could hear the panting and sniffing of the wolves near their sit-rock. The wolves were trying to pick up their scent and would be on them in a few moments.

Rebekah and Jonas noticed a small opening in the middle of the boulder pile and frantically clawed to it hoping to hide in the rocks. The opening was a narrow entrance to a small rock cave formed by the disarray of boulders. Rebekah quickly squeezed backward through the opening. Jonas followed but was stopped when his jacket snagged on one of the jagged rocks that formed the tiny entrance to the cave.

The wolves were at the base of the rocks as Jonas struggled to get his jacket free. A wolf jumped up on the rocks and Jonas could feel hot wolf-breath on his hand. Just as the wolf tried to bite him, Jonas jerked his hand back into the arm of his jacket. The wolf got a mouth full of sleeve and tried to pull the jacket and Jonas out from between the rocks. Rebekah had grabbed Jonas' feet and was trying to pull him further into the cave. The wolf was winning this tug-of-war until the wolf ripped Jonas' jacket cuff completely off. Both Jonas and Rebekah tumbled back into the center of the rock pile.

They scrambled to the back of the shallow cave and huddled together. They could hear the snarls of the angry wolves as they clawed around the rocks outside.

Jonas looked at his torn jacket.

"Mom's not going to be happy when she sees this," Jonas said as he shoved his ripped sleeve in front of him for Rebekah to see.

Rebekah wasn't looking at Jonas' sleeve. She was watching the entrance to the rock cave as a wolf tried to squeeze through the opening. It was a large dark gray wolf that couldn't get his shoulders through the small entrance. After a couple of tries, he disappeared from view.

They heard more howling and snarling. Then a brown wolf tried to get at them. This wolf was a little smaller but still couldn't get his shoulders through the opening. The brown wolf had crazy, yellow eyes and long white teeth. The brown wolf backed out of the entrance and there was more howling and snarling.

Then a gray and white wolf tried to get through the cave entrance. This wolf was so quiet it was creepy; it made no growls or snarls—it just glared at Rebekah and Jonas with squinty, cold, empty blue eyes as it wriggled half way through the entrance.

Rebekah and Jonas didn't know what to do. The wolves had secured the only way out of the rock cave. Jonas wished he had brought a walking stick with him. His dad had always said it was a good idea to bring one up in the brush. If he had one, he could have poked and wacked any wolf that tried to come through the narrow cave opening.

Rebekah suggested they pray to ask God to get them out of this mess. They tried to ignore the snarls of the wolves as they joined hands to ask God for quick help. They hadn't been praying more than a few minutes when the meanest, loudest, scariest roar blasted through the rocks and seemed to shake the ground they were sitting on.

The grey and white wolf stopped inching toward Rebekah and Jonas. Its empty blue eyes were now open wide with fear. All of a sudden the wolf jerked back once—then again—and then disappeared in an instant. Something had yanked it back through the rocks.

They could hear a fierce fight going on outside. Wolves were snarling and snapping their teeth together. Something else would growl menacingly and give one of those ground-shaking roars in response. Rebekah and Jonas crawled toward the entrance to the cave to take a peek at what was happening out there. They heard a roar, a yelp, and then saw through the cave opening a wolf flying through the air. The roars, growls, and yelps continued for a few minutes, and then there was quiet.

Almost Made It Through

# Chapter 2:

# Wall of Trees

It took Rebekah and Jonas several minutes to muster the courage to inch through the narrow cave entrance and peak outside. When they did, they were stunned by what they saw. Instead of rock and brush, they were looking at a beautiful, quiet snow covered pine forest.

Jonas looked at Rebekah – only his head, arms and shoulders poking out of the rock cave.

"We don't have this many pine trees on our property, and it doesn't snow this much either."

As Rebekah squatted just outside the cave entrance, she grabbed a handful of the white stuff, squeezed it, and brought it closer to her face for a better look.

"Maybe we should stay inside the cave for a while," suggested Jonas. "Those animals could still be around."

"I think the wolves and that 'roar thing' are gone," said Rebekah as she stood up and brushed the snow off her hand on her jacket. "We should look around to see if we can figure out where we are."

Jonas left the safety of the cave entrance and scooted down the rocks into the snow next to Rebekah. It was ankle deep and smooth as a fitted bed sheet except for near the front of the cave. Where they were standing, the snow was trounced, and they could see splotches of blood and mud in the snow— evidence of the fight they had heard a little while ago. There were too many wolf tracks to count, but there was one set of tracks that stood out. They must have belonged to the 'roar-thing.'

"Look at the size of those tracks!" exclaimed Jonas.

Rebekah stepped into one of the big tracks. It was twice as long and three times as wide as Rebekah's boot—not counting the long claw marks.

Rebekah and Jonas looked at each other and at the same time said, "Bear!"

"There aren't supposed to be bears on our property," said Jonas.

"I don't think this is our property…anymore," replied Rebekah hesitantly as she stared at the tracks.

"How can that be?" asked Jonas. "We didn't go anywhere."

Rebekah looked in the direction where their house should have been and saw only a wall of trees. In fact, they were surrounded by a wall of trees except for a wide winding path that disappeared going into the trees north of them. There were bear tracks in the snow as far up the path as they could see.

"It looks like that's the only path out of here," said Rebekah, nodding at the path to the north. "Maybe we should follow it for a while to see where it goes."

"I don't want to meet up with that bear!" exclaimed Jonas.

"I don't want to have another meeting with those wolves," countered Rebekah. "I think we should get out of here and that path is the only trail to follow."

"I guess dealing with one bear might be better than dealing with a whole pack of wolves," reasoned Jonas. "Maybe he won't bother us. He fought off the wolves and left. He didn't try to get us."

"I think maybe he just doesn't like wolves," said Rebekah. "And he may not have known we were in the rocks. I hope we don't run into either of them."

"Let's follow the path," conceded Jonas. "It doesn't look like we have much choice. At least we'll be moving. I'm freezing."

So Rebekah and Jonas started walking up the path through the pine trees. After walking several minutes, they realized how quiet the forest was. No bird sounds. No squirrel sounds. No any kind of sounds except their feet crunching in the snow. The path headed steadily up the mountain that should have been the hill behind their house.

They walked for what seemed like a long time before the path leveled off a bit. Soon the path forked and Rebekah and Jonas were faced with another decision. The path to the north continued up the mountain and looked just like the one they had been following. The other path branched off to the west and went downhill.

"Which way should we go?" asked Jonas.

"Well, I'm tired of walking uphill, my feet are cold, and we're walking away from where our house is supposed to be. Let's go down."

"But we already know our house isn't where it's supposed to be," said Jonas, "and we haven't seen wolf tracks since we started up here."

"That's strange," said Rebekah, distracted from Jonas' remarks. "The bear tracks end here. Look, they come up right to the fork in the path and stop."

Jonas looked back down the path and eyed the bear tracks as far back as he could see them. He then looked at the ground in front of him and couldn't see where the bear had gotten off the path.

"How could the bear tracks just stop?" muttered Rebekah half under her breath.

"He must have gone into the woods from here," surmised Jonas.

"There are no tracks going off into the woods. They just stop here in the middle of the path." Rebekah slowly looked around. "This isn't right. I think we should get out of here. Let's go downhill."

"Home has to be down there somewhere," said Jonas.

As they both turned to start down the path to the west, they heard something moving in the trees to their right. They looked toward the movement and saw what looked like a very large boulder rising up from the ground. Before they could take more than a few steps, a huge silver grizzly bear moved out of the trees and blocked their way. The bear was so close that they could feel his breath on their faces. The bear stared at them—as if he were waiting to see what they were going to do next. Rebekah and Jonas stared back, but only because they didn't know what else to do. They knew they couldn't outrun the bear, and they knew they couldn't fight it. Knowing what they couldn't do was not helping them decide what they should do.

Finally, Jonas whispered to Rebekah, "Maybe we should try to scare him."

"How?" Rebekah whispered back.

"Let's jump up and down and act crazy—that might make him run away," Jonas offered.

"It might also make him mad," Rebekah added

"I remember reading a story about Davy Crockett staring a bear to death. Maybe we can do that."

"How long did it take to…Jonas! That's just a tall tale. This is not the time for joking around," whispered Rebekah in an exasperated tone.

"I'm not joking," said Jonas defensively. "It worked in the book."

"That was just a story, Jonas. It didn't really happen like that."

"How do **you** know?" retorted Jonas.

As they were debating this issue, Jonas thought he saw the bear start to smile. Rebekah only saw teeth and thought they were about to be eaten.

The bear spoke.

"How did you two get into Treetop?" asked the silver bear who had a very deep voice. "People aren't supposed to be in Treetop."

Rebekah and Jonas just stood there staring at the bear. Bears weren't supposed to talk. For a few moments they were too stunned to speak. The bear waited for an answer.

"Bears aren't supposed to talk. How come you can talk?" asked Jonas hesitantly.

"All animals in Treetop can talk," answered the silver bear. "You're not supposed to be in Treetop to hear us. How did you get here?"

"We don't know how we got here" answered Jonas. "We were

drinking hot cocoa and watching clouds on our sit-rock at home when the wolves came."

"Yeah," said Rebekah, finally able to speak. "And when we ran to our rock fort, it wasn't our rock fort. It was a pile of rocks with a cave in the middle…"

Jonas cut in, "And the wolves tried to get us in the rock fort—I mean rock cave—and we thought we were done for…"

Rebekah interrupted Jonas this time, "and then the wolves got into a fight and we heard snarling and big roars and after a few minutes everything got quiet and then we peeked out of the cave…and everything had changed."

There was silence for a moment as Rebekah and Jonas again tried to make sense of what they had just told the bear. The silver bear waited patiently for them to continue their story.

"When we looked out from the rock cave, we saw a pine forest covered in snow. The problem is—we don't have a pine forest and snow at our home," said Jonas.

"And we looked to where our house was supposed to be, but it wasn't there—just trees were there." Rebekah's voice trailed off as she finished their story. She and Jonas realized now more than ever that they were really lost and that made them sad. And they were talking to a bear! Things couldn't have been more mixed up.

"I know you have to be confused and probably a little frightened, but I think I might be able to help you. We'll find a way to get you back home," said the bear in a very soothing tone.

Jonas had been checking out the bear as Rebekah and the bear were talking, and he noticed a little blood on his left front leg. He nudged Rebekah and nodded for her to look at the blood just as the bear had finished speaking.

When Rebekah saw the blood, she blurted out, "You fought the wolves this morning, didn't you?" Without waiting for him to answer, she asked, "Were you fighting them to help us or did you fight them because you just don't like wolves? Did they hurt you? Did you kill…"

The silver bear cut Rebekah off in mid-sentence, "I like wolves," he said, "I just don't like those particular wolves. You were on the border of Treetop in that rock cave of yours. I am one of the guardians of Treetop, and it was my obligation to protect you from those bad wolves."

"How did you know we needed help?" asked Jonas. "You came just in time—I thought that grey and white wolf was going to squeeze into the cave and get us. I thought we were goners."

"You prayed, didn't you?" asked the silver bear.

Rebekah and Jonas nodded.

The silver bear continued, "Didn't you expect your prayer to be heard?"

"I know that God hears them," replied Rebekah, "but I don't think He always answers them right away."

"Yeah," said Jonas, "My dad said God answers when He answers – not when we think He should."

"Hmm," said the silver bear, "that's wisdom most creatures don't attain."

Rebekah remembered their prayer and how they had heard the earth-shaking roar even before they had finished it.

"But it seems like this time God did answer right away," said Rebekah.

"Yeah," chimed in Jonas, "you were in the right place at the right time for us."

"It seems I had a little help, doesn't it?" chuckled the silver bear.

Their conversation with the bear was interrupted by a squeaky little voice behind them, "What are those things?" it asked.

Rebekah and Jonas both turned around and looked to see who was speaking, but they saw no one.

"They are people," answered the silver bear. "Little people—children to be exact."

"I've heard of them, and none of what I heard was much good! What are they doing here?" demanded the squeaky voice.

When the squeaky voice spoke the second time, Rebekah and Jonas tracked it to a large pine at the fork in the path. It was coming from a large grey squirrel on a branch about twelve feet off the ground.

"They don't know what they are doing here or how they got here," answered the silver bear. "They are going to need some help finding their way back home."

"Children, this is Mr. Nuttybuddy. He is not as unfriendly as he sounds. He helps keep an eye on things in Treetop. And I am Silver Bear. What are your names?"

"I'm Rebekah and this is my brother, Jonas. I'm seven years old and he's six. We live on Bell Rock Road. Do you know where that is?"

"I know there is no place by that name in Treetop," said Silver Bear. "Ever hear of a place called Bell Rock Road, Mr. Nuttybuddy?" asked Silver Bear.

"Nope," answered Mr. Nuttybuddy, "and I'm not sure there is such a place. Better keep an eye on those two, Silver Bear. I wouldn't trust 'em until I know 'em, and I hope they don't stay in Treetop long enough for me to know 'em. Trouble follows for animals when people show up in a place. I don't want no trouble in Treetop—none at all!"

"I have a notion that Rebekah and Jonas will bring no trouble to anyone in Treetop," replied Silver Bear.

"Children, I think it best you follow me up the path to my house. You can rest there, and maybe we can come up with a plan to get you back home. What do you say?"

Rebekah and Jonas conferred with each other for a minute. Rebekah turned back to Silver Bear. "Our parents told us—-we're not supposed to go anywhere with strangers," Rebekah said hesitantly.

Silver Bear got that bear smile on his face again, but it didn't scare Rebekah this time.

"That's a good thing to be taught." conceded Silver Bear, "but they were referring to people strangers. Did they ever say anything about talking bears?" Silver Bear's smile seemed to get wider.

Rebekah smiled back, "No, they didn't say anything about talking bears." Rebekah paused, looked at Jonas and added, "I guess we can use some help. We don't know where we are going or how to get back home."

"Then follow me, and we'll get you some help," said Silver Bear, and he turned and started to lumber up the path.

**"How did you two get into Treetop?"**

# Chapter 3:

# Maybe They're Spies!

Rebekah and Jonas followed Silver Bear up the mountain. The path was steep, but the country was beautiful. The path leveled off a bit after about a half hour of climbing. At that point, it became narrower and forked again. Silver Bear stopped at the fork and sat down. Rebekah and Jonas walked up beside him and stopped.

"We'll rest here for a few minutes," Silver Bear said.

Rebekah and Jonas were very tired and welcomed the rest. They climbed up on a big rock just off the path and sat down.

"There are a few things you should learn right away about Treetop in case you ever wander around on your own—which I don't advise you to do," Silver Bear said as he sat down beside the big rock. "You must remember that any path leading out of Treetop is a bad path to follow. That's why I blocked your way down at the fork in the road. The path you were going to take leads to Rustcoat—a miserable land of sand, heat, saltwater, and bad animals. Some of the animals there were in Treetop long ago, but they were rebellious and were forced to leave. Those wolves that attacked you this morning came from Rustcoat."

"The animals that were forced out of Treetop were an ornery, arrogant bunch of troublemakers, and I can't say that I was sorry to see them go. They were warned to make right choices, but they wouldn't listen.

Now, after years of living in that miserable Rustcoat, they are not only ornery and arrogant, but resentful and angry, too."

Silver Bear looked directly at Rebekah and Jonas; his soft eyes became very serious—almost hard. He warned, "You don't ever want to take a path that leads to Rustcoat. Those who go to Rustcoat are not welcome back to Treetop."

"My dad has talked about a place he called Rustcoat. He said Rustcoat was a place where coast people lived and that things rusted there because of the stinkin' salt air. We didn't know that any paths here led there," said Rebekah.

Silver Bear smiled and said, "What your dad said about Rustcoat is true for some of it."

"How are we to know which paths are good ones and which ones are bad?" asked Jonas.

"Any path that leads out of the snow covered pines is a path not to follow," answered Silver Bear. "We have a little saying in Treetop to help those who need reminding which paths to avoid. It goes like this:

*Not all paths are good for travel.*
*Don't take a long walk on sand or gravel.*
*All paths level and climbing are right.*
*If you can keep snow, fir, and pine trees in sight.*

"If you do what the saying says, you will stay in Treetop. Fail to obey its wisdom, and you will end up in Rustcoat," warned Silver Bear.

Rebekah and Jonas thought about what the saying meant. Rebekah spoke, "But if we follow the saying, we will never find our house. You see, we can't keep snow and pines in sight and still get home. We don't get snow at home, and unless we plant them, pine trees are scarce there."

"If there is no snow or pines where you live, why do you live there?" asked a surprised Silver Bear.

"I'm not sure why we live where we live, but we can't follow your saying and get there—that's for sure," answered Rebekah. "Our house is down from here. If we are going to get back home, we can't take climbing paths—we have to go downhill."

Silver Bear was frowning when Rebekah finished her explanation. "That's not good to hear. All paths out of Treetop head downhill…and all of them end up in Rustcoat. It's hard to believe your family would have you live in Rustcoat. Rustcoat is a despicable place full of all that is unpleasant."

There was a long pause as Silver Bear thought about Rebekah's and Jonas' situation. Then he said, "I'm going to need some help to find your home. Let's get started again. We don't have much farther to go before we can rest comfortably and have something to eat."

"Mr. Nuttybuddy, I know you're still listening up there somewhere," said Silver Bear glancing up in the trees. "Would you please go on ahead and let Mrs. Silver Bear know I am bringing some guests home. Tell her we should arrive in about half an hour."

"Maybe they're spies!" accused Mr. Nuttybuddy directly above them. "Are you sure you want to bring them into the Circle without getting to know more about them. They all but admitted they live in Rustcoat. Nothing good comes out of Rustcoat!"

"I wouldn't have been sent to help them if they weren't His children," said Silver Bear. "It will be alright. Now, off with you."

Mr. Nuttybuddy made a chatter that didn't sound like he agreed with Silver Bear. "I'll tell Mrs. Silver Bear. I'll tell her alright! I'll tell her the Rustcoats are coming! That's what I'll tell her."

And with that, Mr. Nuttybuddy disappeared in the tree—off on his assignment.

Silver Bear sighed and shook his head as Mr. Nuttybuddy left for his home. "He really is a nice squirrel," said Silver Bear. "A bit overcautious maybe, but he does mean well."

Silver Bear stood up and said, "No more steep climbs for a while— just a nice level stroll. You are now in Treetop Circle. I believe you are the first children to ever visit here. I hope you like it."

They continued to follow Silver Bear along the snow covered path that meandered through the pine and fir trees. It was a crisp, clear morning and from high in the trees, Rebekah, Jonas, and Silver Bear looked like a short train winding through the forest—their frosty breath looking like smoke from a steam engine.

For a little while, Rebekah and Jonas forgot their troubles and became engrossed in trying to jump from one of Silver Bear's tracks to the other without touching the snow in between. Silver Bear had long strides, so it was not an easy thing for them to do. Rebekah and Jonas would giggle each time one of them missed the track or slipped and fell into the snow.

It had been a long time since that forest had heard human laughter.

After a while, Silver Bear made a right turn off the main path and started down a smaller trail that ran between two huge boulders. After a short walk down that trail, it dead-ended at a steep grass covered hill. There was a large arched timber door embedded in the hillside with two curtained windows on each side of it and one above it. A warm, cheery light streamed from the windows onto the snowy forest floor. There was a smoking chimney on each side of the second story window.

Silver Bear went up to the door, opened it, stood aside, and gestured for them to enter. "Welcome to my home. Come in and rest for a while."

Rebekah and Jonas could hardly believe they were actually visiting a bear's home. When they walked through the door, they saw a kitchen off to their left. There were two pots and a tea kettle warming on the wood stove. The tasty smells from the kitchen started to make them hungry.

Off to their right was a cozy sitting room with four big stuffed chairs—two on each side of a beautiful stone fireplace. The chairs were placed on the edge of a thick tan carpet that ran up to the edge of the hearth. Past the sitting room in the middle of the hallway was a stairway leading up to a second level in the house. Beyond the stairway there were two more doorways on each side of the hall.

As soon as they had taken this all in, another huge grizzly bear appeared on the upper hallway to the left of the stairway and looked down on them. This bear was dark brown—almost black—with beautiful silver streaks running along the sides of its body.

"I'm so glad you're back safe, dear. I was worried about you having to leave so quickly to handle the emergency." She looked at the children and smiled. "Were these children your emergency?" she asked as she started down the stairs.

"They were. Mrs. Silver Bear, meet Rebekah and Jonas of Bell Rock Road. They are lost for the moment, a bit scared I suspect, and quite hungry for sure. They have had quite a morning and a very long hike. Did Mr. Nuttybuddy tell you we were coming?"

"Yes, he told me you were coming, but at first he would only tell me you were coming with Rustcoats and that he didn't approve of it one bit. I finally calmed him down with some warm acorn tea, and he told me you were coming home with some children with a suspicious story about how they came to be in Treetop. He does get worked up over things, doesn't he?" smiled Mrs. Silver Bear.

Mrs. Silver Bear turned to Rebekah and Jonas. "Welcome to our home, Rebekah and Jonas of Bell Rock Road. Why don't you two come into the kitchen and have a seat at the table. I will get some food for your tummies and something to drink. Then you can rest for a while."

Rebekah and Jonas followed Mrs. Silver Bear into the kitchen and sat at the kitchen table. They noticed that the room was very Christmassy. The table cloth had a holly design on it; the candle in the middle of the table had a small pine wreath around it; all the tea cups, mugs, and plates on the numerous shelves were various combinations of red, green, white, and gold—with holly or Christmas trees on them. The curtains on the windows were made of white lacy material with tiny fir trees embroidered around the borders. It was a very pleasant room.

Mrs. Silver Bear set two steaming mugs in front of Rebekah and Jonas. She also placed two plates in front of them with slices of cheeses of all colors, some nuts, some bread, and some honey.

"I think you will like the pine spice tea. It will take the chill right out of you. Help yourself to the food while Mr. Silver Bear and I discuss things in the other room."

Mrs. Silver Bear left the children in the kitchen and joined Mr. Silver Bear who was already sitting in one of the overstuffed chairs by the fireplace. Rebekah and Jonas weren't trying to be nosey, but they could see across the hall into the other room and couldn't help but overhear the conversation.

"How bad was it?" asked Mrs. Silver Bear as she sat in the chair across from Mr. Silver Bear.

"Pretty bad," Silver Bear said very seriously. Five wolves from Rustcoat crossed the border of Treetop and tried to harm the children. Dameon was the leader. Stickers and Weed were with him. I didn't know the other two. Dameon, Stickers, and Weed let the other two wolves do the fighting for them. I think they purposefully brought wolves who knew nothing of the power in Treetop so their meanness wasn't lessened by fear. They were pretty vicious."

"Were you hurt?" Mrs. Silver Bear asked, looking at the blood on his leg.

"That's not mine. I think Dameon will have to find other wolves to help him with his mischief next time. I don't think those two will be back any time soon."

"Next time?" asked Mrs. Silver Bear. "Do you think there will be a 'next time'?"

"I hope not, but I suspect I haven't seen the last of them. I didn't think I'd ever see Dameon and his sidekicks in Treetop again. Finding them today makes me feel very uneasy. Why have they come back now? Why were they after the children? Two things are certain—they were up to no good, and they can't be trusted. We must be watchful," cautioned Silver Bear

"I'll be watchful, but I wouldn't mind the chance to give Weed a piece of my paw. I never did like that sneaky little wolf," said Mrs. Silver Bear disgustedly. "I suppose you will be going to the Summit with this news?" she asked.

"Yes. I don't know where this Bell Rock Road is, and if Dameon does come back, I'll need to know what to do about it. I'm sure he has a plan, I just need to know what it is."

"Will you take the children with you, or leave them here with me?"

"They will come with me. Just in case Dameon tries something, I don't want you to have to worry about the children. As soon as the children finish their food and have a little rest, we'll head out."

Rebekah and Jonas looked at each other over their steaming cups of pine spice tea.

"They knew three of the wolves that attacked us," whispered Rebekah. "I wonder how they knew them."

"I don't know, but we're being taken to the 'Summit'. I wonder where that is," whispered Jonas.

At that moment, Mrs. Silver Bear came back into the kitchen and noticed that the children had eaten all the food put before them.

"Would you like more cheese or bread?" asked Mrs. Silver Bear. "There's plenty more if you're still hungry," she added pleasantly. "How did you like the pine spice tea?"

Both Rebekah and Jonas said they had full tummies and both loved the tea.

"I'm a little tired, though," admitted Rebekah.

"Yeah," said Jonas, "Me, too."

"That's because you walked so far, your tummies are full, and the tea relaxes you. Come, I'll show you where you can rest for a while."

Mrs. Silver Bear led them to a room down the entry hall. It was a comfortable room with a big, overstuffed bed on the far wall. In the far right corner, there was a large fireplace with a low fire burning up some logs.

"You two climb up on the bed and rest for a while. I'll come and check on you in a little bit," Mrs. Silver Bear said as she left the room.

Rebekah and Jonas didn't waste any time getting on the bed. They both laid on their backs staring up at the ceiling and thinking about all that had happened to them that day. Before too long, Rebekah was fast asleep, but Jonas' mind was racing and he couldn't relax.

*I must be dreaming*, he said to himself. *How could we be at a place where bears can talk? Where did our house go? How did the forest spring up around the rock cave – where our rock fort should have been? That pile of rocks that protected us from the wolves was nothing like the rock fort on our property. How can that be?* he wondered to himself.

Jonas sat up on the bed and said out loud this time, "I must be dreaming!" He then took hold of some skin on his arm and pinched himself real hard to wake himself up. He pinched and pinched and pinched until he let out a small, "oww." But nothing changed–he was still sitting on the bed by the fireplace. "I gotta be dreaming," he said out loud again as he flopped back down on the bed. He got so tired trying to figure things out that he finally dozed off next to Rebekah.

**West end of Treetop Circle**

# Chapter 4:

# Waterfall

As Jonas slept, he dreamt of Treetop and the wolves. In his dream, the bad wolves had just gotten into Silver Bear's house and were coming down the hall to get him and Rebekah. The dream was so real, Jonas awoke and bolted to a seated position on the bed looking at the doorway—expecting the wolves to come through it at any second.

"I hope I'm dreaming this time!" Jonas exclaimed.

Instead of wolves, a huge bear poked her head in the doorway with her long, sharp white teeth showing. Jonas about jumped off the bed in fright.

It was Mrs. Silver Bear smiling at him, "Did I hear you say you had a dream, dear?" asked Mrs. Silver Bear. Mrs. Silver Bear noticed that she had frightened Jonas.

"I'm sorry, Jonas. I didn't mean to startle you. You better wake up your sister. It's time for you two to go with Silver Bear to the Summit." And with that Mrs. Silver Bear left and went back down the hall toward the Kitchen.

Jonas shook Rebekah to wake her. She didn't budge. Jonas shook her again—harder this time. "Rebekah, wake up! We've got to go now."

Rebekah mumbled something that sounded like, "Is it Christmas yet?"

"Rebekah, wake up! It's time to go with Silver Bear to the place they call the Summit."

"Silver Bear?—Summit?" It was Rebekah's turn to bolt upright in the bed. "Jonas, I had the strangest dream. We...," she stopped speaking as she looked around the room. It wasn't their room!

She looked at Jonas and then around the room again. "For a second I thought this was all a dream," she said dismally.

Just at that moment, Mrs. Silver Bear stuck her head in the doorway again and smiled. "Good. You are both awake. Did you say you had a dream, too, Rebekah?"

Rebekah's mouth fell open as she stared at Mrs. Silver Bear in the doorway.

"Rebekah, are you alright, dear?" Mrs. Silver Bear asked soothingly.

"She's alright," said Jonas. "She's just not fully awake yet. Sometimes it takes her awhile."

"Well, you have a few minutes before you leave for the Summit. Would you like more to eat or drink before you go?" asked Mrs. Silver Bear.

"No, thank you." replied Rebekah and Jonas.

"Very well, Silver Bear will be coming to get you in a moment."

After Mrs. Silver Bear left them, Rebekah and Jonas sat on the bed for a few minutes—both thinking about their situation. Rebekah spoke first.

"I wonder what is going to happen at this Summit place."

"Yeah, and I wonder who 'he' is." added Jonas.

"He?" Rebekah looked at Jonas quizzically. "He who?"

"The 'he' Silver Bear is going to see at the Summit. Remember when we were in the kitchen, and the bears were talking in the fireplace room? Silver Bear told Mrs. Silver Bear that 'he' would have a plan and that he—Silver Bear—needed to know what it was."

"I do remember that," said Rebekah. "I wonder who 'he' is."

Jonas' eyes narrowed at Rebekah for asking the same question he had just asked her and was about to say something about it when they were interrupted by a voice in the doorway.

"'He' is Christmas Bear," said Silver Bear entering the room. Christmas Bear is the elder bear in Treetop. When Treetoppers have a problem we can't handle or come across something we don't understand, we go to Christmas Bear for help. We will explain your situation to him, and he will tell us what we need to do to make things right."

"Christmas Bear…Christmas Bear. My dad told us a story about a Christmas Bear once," said Rebekah. "He was a huge bear with thick white/silver hair that smelled like pine trees. He delivered gifts to all the forest animals on Christmas Eve. In the story, two puppies named Jabekah and Ronas were lost. Christmas Bear gave them a ride home on his back. That's how the puppies knew his fur smelled like the pines."

Silver Bear stared at Rebekah for a moment. He thought it an odd coincidence that Rebekah's father's story would be about a Christmas Bear whose fur smelled of pine and who delivered presents to forest animals on Christmas Eve.

"How come you think Christmas Bear can help us?" asked Rebekah, interrupting Silver Bear's thoughts.

"Christmas Bear's wisdom was a gift given to him long ago," answered Silver Bear—divulging nothing more. "Tell me more about this Christmas Bear story your dad made up."

Jonas began to explain, "It was a story about two puppies name Jabekah and Ronas. Get it—Jabekah/Rebekah, Ronas/Jonas? Anyway, these puppies get lost in a forest a lot like Treetop. Wolves try to attack them and they hide in a rock fort. The Christmas Bear scares the wolves off…"

Rebekah interrupted, "But we…I mean Jabekah and Ronas didn't know it was the Christmas Bear right away. They only heard something fighting with the wolves. When Jabekah and Ronas followed the big footprints that led away from the fight with the wolves, they ran into Christmas Bear. He took us…I mean he took Jabekah and Ronas along while he delivered some presents to a few forest animals and then helped Jabekah and Ronas find their home."

Silver Bear just sat there for a moment looking back and forth between Rebekah and Jonas. "Well," he finally said, "it's very strange that what happened to you today is very similar to your dad's story. When did he tell you this story?"

Last year at Christmas time," answered Rebekah.

Silver Bear was thinking about their dad's story and the day's events when Mrs. Silver Bear came to the doorway.

"Dear, it's getting late. You and the children best get going if you want to get to the Summit before dark."

"You're right. We must leave at once," said Silver Bear. "Christmas Bear will be leaving for his visits, and if we miss him we won't be able to see him again until morning. Come along, children. We have quite a climb ahead of us."

Rebekah, Jonas, and Silver Bear left for the Summit without delay. As they left the warmth of Silver Bear's home, the frosty air of Treetop filled their lungs. It felt good and smelled good. Rebekah and Jonas were anxious to get to the Summit and meet this Christmas Bear.

They took the same trail from the house to the main path just beyond the huge boulders they had passed on the way in. They turned right and walked about a mile before Silver Bear turned right again off the path into the forest. Rebekah and Jonas followed Silver Bear as he twisted and turned between the trees. The children soon became disoriented with no path to follow and no landmarks upon which to base their position. Deeper and deeper into the forest they went.

Soon they came to a break in the trees and found themselves in a huge meadow with a trail that headed downhill. As they walked down this trail, Jonas remembered that the Treetop "saying" had warned that only level and climbing paths were good ones.

"Silver Bear," Jonas said, "This path is going downhill. Didn't you warn us that downhill paths lead to Rustcoat?"

"Very good, Jonas!" Silver Bear exclaimed. "I'm pleased that you remembered the saying. But you must remember it exactly, and you must apply it with wisdom. Downhill paths do lead to Rustcoat, but only the ones where you can't keep pine and fir trees in sight. Some of the paths in Treetop incline and decline depending on whether you are climbing one of our mountains or descending into one of our valleys, but you will always be surrounded by pines and firs here. When a path takes you downhill for too long, the pines and firs begin to thin out. It also starts to become warmer. So, if you are going downhill and the pines and firs are thinning and you feel it getting warmer, you should turn around and go in the other direction. Do you both understand the saying a little better now?"

"Yes," replied Rebekah and Jonas, nodding in agreement.

Silver Bear continued, "One more little tip for you to remember. You will notice in Treetop that you can always see your breath. Each time you breathe out, your breath makes a frosty cloud in front of your face. That is a gift given to Treetoppers. It is to remind us to be thankful for every single breath we are able to take. As you get closer to Rustcoat, your breath becomes less visible—and it eventually disappears altogether. Let this be a warning to you. If your breath begins to disappear, you are going in the wrong direction. Be grateful for each breath you take and stay away from places where it cannot be seen so you don't take your breaths for granted."

"We can see our breath at our home sometimes," offered Jonas.

"But most of the time we can't," added Rebekah.

"Seeing it sometimes is better than never seeing it," commented Silver Bear.

They continued on in silence for several minutes. The sun had already gone behind the mountain on their left. As they walked down through the meadow, the valley narrowed quickly. The mountains on either side of them towered high in the sky and were carpeted with pines and firs, but the mountain in front of them and off to the left was a bit smaller, very rocky, and patched with low brushy plants. It was rather odd, in comparison—there were no trees on it.

As they walked along, they heard the rushing sound of water behind the trees. Soon they came upon a large alcove at the base of the mountain on their left. At the back of the alcove was a wide waterfall that tumbled over a rock shelf that was about twenty feet high. The fall was far enough off the path and surrounded on three sides by thick forest so you couldn't see it until you almost passed it. The water from the fall pooled in a sandy area that took up most of the alcove's floor. It was a beautiful place.

"This way," said Silver Bear walking toward the waterfall. "We've still got quite a climb to make, but we're almost there."

Mrs. Silver Bear had watched out the kitchen window until Silver Bear and the Children walked out of sight toward Treetop Circle Path. Then she went out for some air—in the direction of the southern border of Treetop. She had not liked hearing about the bad wolves at Treetop's border, and she was going to make sure they weren't lingering there, or worse–entering Treetop.

It was easy to follow the trail Silver Bear and the Children made to her house. When she came to the place where Silver Bear confronted the children, she heard a noise overhead.

"Mr. Nuttybuddy, are you following me?" Mrs. Silver Bear asked knowingly looking up in the trees.

"No," answered Mr. Nuttybuddy abruptly. "I was coming to get you. While you and Silver Bear entertained those Rustcoats, I went back to where Silver Bear fought with the wolves. I figured those Rustcoats were all in this together. Those "children", as you call them, are a diversion. While Silver Bear gives them a tour of Treetop, their evil pets are planning to sneak back here and do who-knows-what mischief. I tell you there's trouble brewing!"

"Mr. Nuttybuddy, I don't think Rebekah and Jonas are spies, and stop calling them Rustcoats! You know Silver Bear and I have a good sense about character, so don't insult us by suggesting we're reading this situation improperly," admonished Mrs. Silver Bear.

"How do you know for sure?" asked Mr. Nuttybuddy skeptically.

"I don't have to prove them innocent, you have to prove them guilty!" What evidence do you have of them conspiring with bad wolves other than your wild imaginings?"

Mr. Nuttybuddy started to open his mouth, but then shut it without saying anything.

"That's just what I thought," said Mrs. Silver Bear. "Now I want you to stop this gossiping about the children, or I just may not feel like making you acorn tea for a long, long while. How would you like that?"

Mr. Nuttybuddy's eyes got big at Mrs. Silver Bear's threat of cutting him off from her delicious acorn tea. Nobody made it better than Mrs. Silver Bear. "Ok, ok," said Mr. Nuttybuddy. "I'll try."

"You'll try?" scoffed Mrs. Silver Bear.

"I'll stop, I'll stop!" exclaimed Mr. Nuttybuddy.

"That's good of you, Mr. Nuttybuddy," said Mrs. Silver Bear approvingly. "Now, what were you coming to get me for?

Mr. Nuttybuddy's mind had to shift from acorn tea to the business at hand. "They haven't left," he said. "Dameon and Weed are sitting by a rock pile on the south border. They are talking about "trouble" and I heard Skull's name mentioned. I couldn't get close enough to hear all of their conversation."

"Is it just the two of them?" asked Mrs. Silver Bear.

"I didn't see anyone else, and I watched them for quite a while,"

"I'm going to see what they are up to," said Mrs. Silver Bear. Without waiting for Mr. Nuttybuddy to respond, she sprinted down the path toward Treetop's border.

# Chapter 5:

# Last Breath

Rebekah and Jonas followed Silver Bear around the sandy pool on the south side of the waterfall. He got as near to the falls as he could and stared into the water. He then took a long look at Rebekah and Jonas—measuring them up for something.

"You two ever swim under a waterfall?" asked Silver Bear, sounding very cheerful.

Rebekah and Jonas looked at Silver Bear in utter disbelief.

"I thought not," said Silver Bear smiling, "but today you will do just that. We are going to swim under the falls together."

Rebekah and Jonas just stood there looking at Silver Bear—wide-eyed and speechless.

"I know you may find that a little frightening, but I have done this many times. I know you can do it, too. And to ease your minds just a bit, I will do most of the work for you." He paused to let them think about that for a moment.

Rebekah looked up at the waterfall coming over the rocks. Although it was only about twenty feet tall, it looked monstrous when you were close to it. Tons of water were crashing down, and the water at the foot of the falls was all choppy and rough. The noise of the waterfall thundered in their ears. Jonas looked at the pool. It was shallow for about six feet out and then the sand dropped away into a deep, dark blue hole.

Jonas was thinking you would get sucked to the center of the earth if you fell off that sandy ledge. Both he and Rebekah were scared.

"If you do as I say…exactly as I say…everything will be alright," assured Silver Bear. "Now we must get moving. It will be getting dark soon. I want to get through the falls and start our climb. I wouldn't ask you to do something you couldn't do. You have to trust me here." Silver Bear's voice was kind but firm.

"Jonas, get on my left side and grab two handfuls of fur and hold on tight. Rebekah, you get on my right side and do the same."

Rebekah shrugged her shoulders at Jonas and Jonas just shook his head slowly as they each went to opposite sides of Silver Bear.

"I don't suppose there is another way to go to start our climb," stated Jonas numbly.

"I'm afraid not," said Silver Bear. "All other ways are more time consuming, and we don't have time to waste if we want to see Christmas Bear this evening."

"Burrow your hands deep into my fur and grab as much as you can. Go ahead, grab!"

Rebekah and Jonas grabbed some fur and waited.

"Don't worry about hurting me," ordered Silver Bear. "Grab deeper, grab more, grab tighter!"

Rebekah and Jonas dug their fingers deeper into Silver Bear's fur. Being that close to the bear, they noticed the scent of pine in his fur. They both looked at Silver Bear quizzically. Silver Bear just looked back and smiled at them.

"That's good," said Silver Bear. "Now when I count to three, take in a deep breath—on four blow it out and keep blowing it out until I say five. When I get to five, take in another deep breath. When I get to six, let half of that breath out. When I get to seven, take another breath until you can't take in any more air. When I yell, 'NOW!' hold your breath and hang on tight. I'll be diving into the pool at that point. You must hold your breath until we get to the other side of the falls! You must not let go of my fur! Do you both understand me?"

"Yes," said Rebekah and Jonas at the same time. "But that's a lot to remember," added Jonas.

"I'll take you through it one step at a time," consoled Silver Bear.

"Ok, here we go. Hold on tightly. One…two…three—take a breath!"

Rebekah and Jonas took a deeeeep breath.

"Four—blow it all out!" shouted Silver Bear above the roar of the falls.

Rebekah and Jonas blew out all their air and kept trying to blow out more until they heard a "five."

"Five—take in another deep breath!" ordered Silver Bear

Rebekah and Jonas took another deep breath and held it.

"Take in more air!" yelled Silver Bear.

Rebekah and Jonas tried to suck in more air. It was hard, but they managed to do it. Their lungs hurt as they waited to hear "six". There was a pause. Rebekah and Jonas thought their lungs were going to burst. Where was the "six?"

"Six—let half of it out!" shouted Silver Bear

Rebekah and Jonas let half the breath out.

"Seven—take in another breath until it hurts and hold tight!"

Rebekah and Jonas took in a full breath on top of the half breath they were already holding.

"Now!" yelled Silver Bear

Rebekah and Jonas were already holding Silver Bear tightly—so tightly that their hands hurt. But when they heard "Now", they grabbed even tighter. At that very moment, they were both jerked off their feet as Silver Bear ran to the edge of the deep water, leaped, and dove into the base of the falls.

The water was icy cold and very rough. Both Rebekah and Jonas were twisted, pushed and pulled by the churning water. They felt themselves being pulled down deep by Silver Bear. Their ears hurt.

Rebekah opened her eyes but saw nothing but bubbles. She let out some of her breath because she had to. Silver Bear's dive had leveled off. They were now swimming some distance. Rebekah closed her eyes again. There was nothing there she wanted to see.

Jonas had kept his eyes closed during the dive, but as Silver Bear began swimming distance, he opened them. They must have been past the falls because he saw no bubbles except the ones that escaped from his mouth as he let out some of his breath. The water was crystal clear and Jonas saw rock walls all around them. They were in an underwater tunnel!

Silver Bear made an abrupt turn to the right, and Rebekah opened her eyes again just in time to see Silver Bear swim into a hole in the side of the wall. Everything went black. Rebekah couldn't see a thing. She let out a little more breath. She didn't have much breath left!

Jonas had seen the hole in the wall about the same time Rebekah did. It looked scary because it was dark and it looked like it went deeper into the water. Jonas couldn't believe his eyes when he saw Silver Bear swim toward the hole. Everything went black for Jonas, too. He let out a little more of his breath. He didn't have much left either.

The tunnel and the blackness seemed to go on forever. Rebekah and Jonas were both beginning to panic. They were running out of breath and had no idea how long they had to hold out. Their lungs burned. They let out the last breath they had and prayed to God to give them more…somehow.

Rebekah and Jonas felt themselves being jerked upwards. Suddenly, Silver Bear burst through the surface of the water. Rebekah and Jonas gasped in air as Silver Bear climbed onto the rock shore of the cavern they had entered. Silver Bear laid down on his stomach to rest with the two children still clinging to his sides.

After a few moments, their eyes became accustomed to the dimly lit cavern. It was about the size of a big barn with half the floor being water. There was a four foot wide path that started at the water's edge on the south wall and wound its way up the west wall to a doorway on the north wall near the ceiling. Light was entering into the cavern from that doorway.

Silver Bear spoke first. "I told you everything would be alright if you followed my instructions. You did well. Except for being soaking wet, how do you feel?"

"Fine," said Rebekah weakly.

"Ok, I guess" answered Jonas hesitantly.

"Is this the only shortcut to get to the Summit?" asked Rebekah.

"It's the most fun one," answered Silver Bear.

When he saw the disbelieving looks on Rebekah's and Jonas' faces, he added, "It is also the quickest way. We needed to get to the Summit before dark. This was the only way to get there before Christmas Bear starts on his rounds."

"Rounds?" asked Jonas.

"It's when Christmas Bear leaves to go around to the animals in Treetop to give them their Christmas presents," said Silver Bear watching Rebekah and Jonas for their reaction to this news.

"Christmas Bear brings presents to the forest animals?" asked Jonas slowly with eyebrows raised.

"Yes, he does," answered Silver Bear as his gaze rested on Jonas.

"Is it Christmas Eve in Treetop like it was...like it is at home?" asked Jonas.

"It's like Christmas Eve every night in Treetop," answered Silver Bear.

"It's like Christmas Eve every night!" exclaimed Jonas. "How can that be?"

"It's always been that way," said Silver Bear.

"Your fur smells like pine...just like the Christmas Bear in our Daddy's story. Does his fur smell like pine, too?" asked Rebekah inquisitively.

"Yes, it does," answered Silver Bear, starting to get a grin on his face. "Strange isn't it—how Treetop has so many similarities to your Dad's story. The wolves attacking, a bear scaring them away, pine scented fur...it's almost like your Dad has been here before. It's veerrrry strange."

There was silence for a little while as they all pondered these surprising similarities.

"We better get going. We still have quite a climb ahead of us. We should be at the Summit in about an hour. That will give you a few hours with Christmas Bear. Follow me."

Silver Bear got up and started for the path that climbed the sides of the cavern. "Stay close to the wall until we get through the doorway. There's no rail and I don't want you to fall as we get up toward the ceiling."

Rebekah and Jonas followed Silver Bear up the path toward the doorway. They were still soaking wet, but the cavern was strangely warm and they were quite comfortable. Rebekah was staring down at the path in front of her as she wondered if Daddy knew about this place and had been here before. Jonas was humming "Oh Christmas Tree" as he brushed the wall with his hand and wondered why Silver Bear's and Christmas Bear's fur smelled like pine trees. Both were deep in thought as they left the watery cavern.

**Not Just Any Waterfall**

# Chapter 6:

# Summit

Mrs. Silver Bear stopped just before the last bend in the path near the border of Treetop. She stood there and listened. Hearing nothing, she cautiously rounded the bend and caught sight of two wolves lying in the mud at the foot of a rock pile. The wolves hadn't spotted her yet.

"I told you," whispered Mr. Nuttybuddy from above—a little too loudly.

The wolves turned and looked up the road and immediately spotted Mrs. Silver Bear. They both jumped to their feet but neither retreated nor advanced. Bear and wolf stared at one another menacingly.

Mrs. Silver Bear started to walk slowly, silently toward the two wolves. Weed bared his fangs and let out a low growl. Mrs. Silver Bear continued to walk closer.

"What are we going to do, Dameon?" whispered Weed worriedly. Mrs. Silver Bear was about fifty feet away and slowly coming closer.

"Move back to the tree line and get behind one," ordered Dameon.

The two wolves slowly backed up to the trees south of the rock pile and positioned themselves behind two of them. Mrs. Silver Bear continued toward them silently until she reached the edge of the jumble of rocks. She was about twenty-five feet from the wolves – still staring at them coldly.

"I see you are still a coward," said Mrs. Silver Bear looking at the wolf called Weed. Turning her attention to Dameon she said sarcastically, "It must be a wonderful honor being a leader of cowards."

"**Hello** to you, too, Mrs. **Silver** Bear," said Weed disrespectfully. "Long time, no see."

"How dare you enter Treetop," Mrs. Silver Bear said ominously to Dameon.

"Were we in Treetop?" said Dameon in mock surprise. If we were, I apologize. We certainly didn't mean to cause offense. We were just looking for our human companions…"

"I knew it!" said Mr. Nuttybuddy. "I …"

"Hush," ordered Mrs. Silver Bear—not taking her eyes off Dameon.

Dameon looked in the trees and saw Mr. Nuttybuddy. "So, you **have** seen our companions, have you?"

Knowing he should have kept his mouth shut, Mr. Nuttybuddy said nothing further.

"I catch either of you in Treetop, you will never leave it," threatened Mrs. Silver Bear.

"Well, you'll have to catch us in it, won't you?" said Weed. "I mean, I can sit here all day and all night and you can't touch me here, can you?" he said mockingly.

As fast as lightning, Mrs. Silver Bear scooped a boulder off the ground and hurled it at Weed. It struck him on his left hip—the only other part of him other than his head that showed from behind the tree. Weed yelped and disappeared behind the tree completely.

"No need to get violent," said Dameon. "We're leaving…for now, but you tell our 'companions' that we'll be back for them. Would you do that for me?" And with a sneer, Dameon turned and disappeared into the trees. Weed, limping, followed.

Mrs. Silver Bear watched them leave, and when they were out of sight, she looked up at Mr. Nuttybuddy.

"Mr. Nuttybuddy, you need to learn to keep your ears open and your mouth shut. You do just the opposite and it is annoying—especially now. The fact that you had some knowledge of the children has helped those evil creatures in some way. We are not to be partners in evil."

"I'm not a partner in evil!" protested Mr. Nuttybuddy. "I didn't intentionally give them anything. Any information they gleaned from my comment…"

"Mr. Nuttybuddy, your incessant need to justify your ill-feelings toward the children is sin. Your sin has somehow contributed to advancing their evil plans, so that makes you a partner in it—willingly or not," scolded Mrs. Silver Bear.

Mr. Nuttybuddy was convicted by Mrs. Silver Bear's words, and he hung his head in regret.

"Mr. Nuttybuddy, I can tell you are sorry for what you have done," said Mrs. Silver Bear softly. "Learn from it so you don't do it again."

"I am sorry," said Mr. Nuttybuddy. "I will do my best to more careful from now on."

"Good. Now I need your help. Go to the Summit. Get word to Silver Bear about this encounter with Dameon and Weed. These animals are still after the children for some reason. Maybe we can find out why."

"I'll go there directly," said Mr. Nuttybuddy.

Mrs. Silver Bear smiled at Mr. Nuttybuddy. "Hurry on now. When you get back, you can tell me about your trip over some acorn tea."

Mr. Nuttybuddy, relieved that Mrs. Silver Bear had forgiven him (and had invited him for tea!), sped off through the treetops toward the Summit.

As they passed through the cavern doorway, they entered a rock passageway about nine feet high and about seven feet wide. The path spiraled up the mountainside and had window-like holes open to the north that gave them enough light to see their way. They climbed around and around for several minutes before Jonas spoke.

"Silver Bear?"

"Yes, Jonas, what is it?" answered Silver Bear, not slowing his pace as he talked.

"You said that the underwater swim was the most fun shortcut to get to the Summit, but it wasn't much fun for me. It was scary, and I thought I was going to drown."

"That way was never meant for people to travel. I only took you that way because our time is limited, and I figured you could handle the shortest swim."

"Shortest swim!" exclaimed Rebekah. "There is a longer swim?"

Before Silver Bear could answer, they turned into a small room that opened to the right of the path. It had a few large, flat rocks up against the wall below a large, rectangular opening about two feet above the flat rocks. Rebekah and Jonas ran to the flat rocks to take a peek out that opening.

"Careful over there," cautioned Silver Bear. "We're pretty high up."

Rebekah and Jonas had no idea how high up they were until they peered out the opening. They were looking out at the cliff side of the Summit. They were so high up that looking down the cliff made Jonas feel funny in his tummy. Rebekah held on to the beveled ledge and looked down thousands of feet to the flatlands below the cliff. It made her feel a little dizzy, too.

"We're at 9,700 feet here. That's Rustcoat down there," said Silver Bear—nodding down to the light and dark brown patches at the base of the mountain. "We were at about 7,500 feet at the waterfall. You couldn't see the cliff side of the mountain from there, but just beyond the trees north of the pool is the northern border of Treetop. Except to the south and a small section west, steep mountain cliffs define Treetop on three sides. The rocky, barren mountain you see below off to the right—you saw just the top of it as we approached the falls—that's Mt. Ugga. It was part of the Treetop Mountains at one time, but long ago a big earthquake split the mountain range. The intermittent aftershocks that followed the main quake further withered that mountain. Nothing of beauty has lived on it since.

Silver Bear turned from the window and laid down next to one of the flat rocks. Rebekah and Jonas sat on the rock next to him.

"So, what's this about there being a 'longer swim' to the cavern? Why the secret swim tunnels to the secret cavern to the secret stairway to get to the Summit?" asked Rebekah—trying to make sense of these new experiences.

Silver Bear smiled. "There is nothing secret about any of this. These places are well known to Treetoppers. They were made for play."

"Play!" exclaimed Jonas. "It almost killed us!"

"Ah, you must remember I told you they were not meant for people." explained Silver Bear.

"Who were they meant for?" asked Rebekah.

"They were made mostly for water creatures–like otters and beavers. They are easy swims for them and provide them with great enjoyment."

"How did you cut through all that rock to make the water tunnels? How did you do it underwater?" asked Jonas.

Silver Bear looked at Rebekah and Jonas. After a pause, he said, "We didn't make them. We could never do anything like that. God made them for us. Then a little smile crossed his face as he added, "He loves us a little too, you know."

Before Rebekah and Jonas were able to think up more questions, Silver Bear got up and said, "We're rested enough, we must get moving." As he headed toward the passageway he called over his shoulder, "Head 'em up, move 'em out."

Jonas whispered to Rebekah, "That's what Dad says when we're going someplace!"

Rebekah acknowledged Jonas' observation with a glance as they both followed Silver Bear up the path.

After several more minutes of climbing, Jonas asked, "Silver Bear, how much farther before we get to the Summit?"

Just as Jonas finished his question, they rounded the last bend in the path. They exited a doorway and stood on a slab of stone before a big snow field. It was early evening. There were so many stars and such a bright full moon that the whole mountainside was lit up with a soft, sparkly glow.

They could see that the field ended about a hundred yards to their right at the cliff side of the mountain. Behind them, in front of them, and to their left the mountain gradually rose another thousand feet. It was like they were standing in the center of a bowl that had been cut in half.

The surrounding slopes were covered with the largest pine trees Rebekah and Jonas had ever seen. The base of their trunks were unbelievably huge, and the trees were at least a hundred-fifty feet tall.

Silver Bear watched with delight as Rebekah and Jonas took in the sight of this breathtaking place. Everywhere they looked was accompanied by their "ohhhhhs" and "ahhhhhs" of wonder. They had heard of enchanted forests in storybooks, and now it seemed as though they were in one.

"We have arrived," said Silver Bear.

**Weed Exposure**

# Chapter 7:

# Mission Failure

Skull sat on a large rock watching two wolves walking towards his hill. One wolf was limping badly. Now he knew for sure that the mission had failed, and his anger started to flare all over again.

Earlier in the day, Stickers, a small but ferocious wolf, had returned to the hill with the bad news. Skull had lost his temper and attacked Stickers. Luckily for Stickers, he was able to out maneuver the larger wolf, and he ran off to wait for Skull's rage to pass.

The hair on Skull's back bristled up as the two wolves approached the camp. He was trying desperately not to show his anger, but he could feel he was losing his struggle.

Dameon and Weed had walked all morning with no rest. The going was slow because of Weed's injury. Dameon stopped at the foot of the barren hill to let Weed catch up. He looked up the slope and saw a large black figure on a rock about three quarters up. It was Skull—waiting… watching. He also knew Skull had a very bad temper. He didn't want to fight the older wolf, partly out of respect and partly because he wasn't sure he could beat him. He and Skull were the largest wolves in the pack.

The only way the other wolves could tell them apart was the slightest trace of silver in Skull's coat.

"He's going to be angry," said Dameon. "Let me do the talking."

"What do you think he's going to do?" asked Weed. Dameon could hear the fear in Weed's voice.

"If you whine and start making excuses, he'll probably lose control of himself and try to tear you to pieces — so keep your mouth shut."

Weed was glad he was with Dameon. Dameon was the only wolf Skull showed any respect for. If anyone could calm Skull, it was Dameon.

Skull remained motionless as he watched the two wolves start up the hill. He couldn't say he liked Dameon because he didn't like anybody. However, he did know that Dameon was no slacker. If he needed something important done, he always sent Dameon.

The two wolves stopped at the foot of the rock that Skull was lying on. Dameon and Stickers waited for Skull to start the conversation. There was a long silence as the wolves stared at each other. Dameon sat down and waited. Weed was afraid to move.

"I suppose you have a good excuse for failure," chided Skull.

"There is an explanation," said Dameon flatly.

Another long silence followed. Weed was fidgety.

"Well, Weed," said Skull – ignoring Dameon, "I'm sure you have some excuses for your failure. What are they?"

Weed hated Skull—as did most of the other wolves. He was arrogant, demeaning, and merciless. Weed waited for Dameon to speak since Dameon had ordered him to keep his mouth shut.

"The bears knew we were coming," said Dameon. "Silver Bear surprised us as we were about to grab the children. The two Rustcoaters with us fought with Silver Bear. Have any of them returned?"

Skull shook head, "No."

"I didn't think so," continued Dameon, "I sent Stickers to you immediately to let you know that the Children entered Treetop. Weed and I waited at the border to see if the children would come back to try to find their home. Instead of the children coming back, Mrs. Silver Bear paid us a visit. Weed was injured when he gave Mrs. Silver some of his lip. She didn't seem to know why the Children were in Treetop. I know she saw them, because that irritating little squirrel Nuttybuddy let it slip. We came here directly after our altercation with Mrs. Silver Bear."

Skull knew he wouldn't have been able to do any better dealing with the bears, so he refrained from berating Dameon and Weed any further.

"Dameon, see that all the wolves in the area are assembled here for a meeting in two hours. Now that the Children are in Treetop, we must move quickly."

**More Bad News**

# Chapter 8:

# The Cottage

Rebekah and Jonas were standing at the doorway of the climb tunnel admiring the quiet and beauty of the mountain when Jonas noticed a quick movement out of the corner of his eye as a shadowy thing swooped closely over their heads. Jonas instinctively ducked to avoid whatever it was, and Rebekah was startled by Jonas' sudden movement. Then Rebekah was startled by the shadowy thing passing over her. Silver Bear didn't move a muscle. The shadowy thing came to rest behind them on top of the climb tunnel's entryway.

"Silver Bear, it's good to see you. You made good time!" said the emotionless voice on top of the Rock.

"Greetings to you, Talon. It is I who am glad to see you." answered Silver Bear.

Rebekah and Jonas looked up to the top of the entryway and saw the biggest eagle they had ever seen! It had a snowy white head on top of a body of silver, black and gray feathers. Its legs were stout and its talons glistened in the moonlight as they curled over the stone edge. It looked magnificent and frightening all at the same time.

"Children, this is Talon. He is the Arch-Eagle of Treetop," said Silver Bear.

Rebekah was stunned by the sight of the great eagle and could only nod a greeting to him.

"Hi," said Jonas timidly as he stared up at the big bird.

Talon nodded to the children but didn't say anything. He just stared at them.

"Talon or one of his lieutenants always meets those who come to the Summit. No one comes or goes here without their permission," explained Silver Bear. Then Silver Bear added, "So, what do you think, Talon, should we allow Rebekah and Jonas to see more of the Summit?"

Now Rebekah and Jonas had not seen Silver Bear wink at Talon when he asked that last question.

Talon jumped down from the entryway and landed right at Rebekah's feet. Rebekah jumped back in surprise and knocked into Jonas. They both fell back and ended up sitting in the snow. Talon looked down at the children. They couldn't pick up any emotion in his black eyes. His large beak curled down into what looked like a fearsome scowl.

"I don't know, Silver Bear," said Talon slowly, "They seem a little skittish. How did they do at the pool?"

"They followed instructions precisely—even when they were scared out of their wits," said Silver Bear smiling, but Rebekah and Jonas did not see his smile either. They couldn't take their eyes off that eagle.

"Well, let's see how they do here." Talon looked back and forth between Rebekah and Jonas for a few moments. "STAND UP!" screeched Talon. "You're sitting in snow!" he shouted. "You're already cold and wet, and now you're getting colder and wetter—on your feet!"

Rebekah and Jonas were startled by Talon's order to "Stand up!" When he shouted, "On your feet!!" they instantly jumped up and were standing face to face with the bird. Their frosty breath crashed into his frosty breath as they stared into the eagle's black marble eyes.

*Boy, this bird is big*, thought Jonas.

*Boy, this bird is mean*, thought Rebekah.

After about a half dozen breaths, Talon addressed Silver Bear but never took his eyes off the children.

"A little jumpy, but they recover quickly—shot right up." There was pause. "Observant, too." There was another pause. "This one here", nodding toward Jonas, "Thinks I'm big, and that one," nodding to Rebekah, "thinks I'm mean."

Rebekah and Jonas thought simultaneously, *this bird can read minds?*

Talon then addressed Rebekah and Jonas, "You are three times right. I am big for an eagle, and I can be mean if I have to be. And, yes, I can hear your thoughts in Treetop. That's something you should remember."

Talon then opened his huge wings and with one stroke, he was back on top of the stone entryway. "Silver Bear, would you mind escorting Rebekah and Jonas to the cottage? I will fly ahead and let Christmas Bear know you have arrived."

Without waiting for an answer, Talon launched off the entryway and soon disappeared over the trees.

"Come on, children," called Silver Bear as he began to walk across the meadow toward the trees behind which Talon had disappeared. "You'll freeze out here in those damp clothes if you stand around here much longer."

Rebekah and Jonas had been too distracted with the beauty of the Summit and the unexpected visit by Talon to pay much attention to how cold it was. Now that Silver Bear mentioned the cold, they both realized their clothes were becoming stiff as the moisture in them froze in the night air. They both started to shiver.

"Well, come on!" encouraged Silver Bear looking over his shoulder at the children. "If you start moving, you'll warm up a bit. We don't have too much farther to go."

Rebekah and Jonas started following Silver Bear. Both were wondering just how far "not too much farther" was. As they entered the trees, it got very dark. They could hardly see the sky through the dense boughs of the huge pines. Silver Bear had slowed his pace so they could easily keep him in view. The snow was not too deep for a huge bear, but it was getting up past Jonas' knees and it made for slow going. They had to follow in Silver Bear's trail to keep up.

After quite a hike, the mountainside leveled off a bit and the forest became less dense. At this level spot, Silver Bear stopped and sat in the snow. The children walked up to him and stopped at his shoulders. You could see the stars again, and the moonlight lit the area with a dull glow. It was a very peaceful place.

"You'll have to go on up from here by yourselves," said Silver Bear very quietly.

Rebekah and Jonas didn't know how to respond at first. They both knew they didn't want to go anywhere by themselves, so they just stood there without saying anything.

"Walk up to the right side of that huge tree in front of us…the biggest one. Walk up there and tell me what you see," said Silver Bear, still in a very quiet voice.

A little bit ahead of them was the biggest tree they had seen so far. It was big even for this forest. The trunk had to be fifteen feet wide, and its gnarled roots reached far out from the base of the tree. It was so tall the top of the tree looked like it touched the sky.

"Go on," Silver Bear said gently. "Tell me what you see."

Rebekah and Jonas didn't particularly want to leave Silver Bear's side, but they didn't want to disobey him either. They grabbed each other's hand for balance and encouragement, and started pushing through the deep snow toward the right side of the tree. They had to pick their steps carefully as some of the huge roots pushed almost a foot above ground and most of them were hidden in the snow. As they rounded the right side of the tree—staying about twenty feet away—they noticed a hollowed out area in the trunk. It was dimly lit, and they could see the beginning of some stairs winding up inside the tree's trunk.

Their eyes slowly scanned up the tree. About thirty feet up there were huge, evenly spaced branches. These branches were bigger than the trunks of normal pine trees. On the back side of the tree on the largest branch, they could see the top of a little white house with a red roof. On the roof was a brown chimney with two big red rings around it. Smoke was coming out the top. They could hardly believe their eyes.

Rebekah, not being able to take her eyes off the smoking chimney, whispered loudly, "Silver Bear, we see a stairway in the tree and a house up in the branches!"

Jonas added in a loud whisper, "It looks like somebody's home! There is smoke coming out of the chimney."

"Go ahead. Go ahead up the stairs and go into the cottage," said Silver Bear softly.

"We want you to come with us," whispered Rebekah.

"Yeah, come with us, Silver Bear," echoed Jonas.

"I have other tasks I must attend to. On with you," urged Silver Bear. "There is no time to waste."

Silver Bear then turned around and hurried back into the trees from which they had come. He was gone before Rebekah and Jonas could protest.

Rebekah and Jonas stood there and stared at the place where Silver Bear had disappeared. They were all alone. The coldness of the night and their frozen clothes made them feel extremely cold. They both looked at the stairs and then up at the cottage.

"It does look kind of cozy up there," said Rebekah.

"I've always wanted to have a tree house just like that one," said Jonas. "Let's go check it out. It can't be a scary place or Silver Bear wouldn't have told us to go up there."

So Rebekah and Jonas walked up to the base of the tree and peered into the hollow trunk. The stairs spiraled up into the tree and were dimly lit, but they couldn't tell what lit them. They looked at each other, shrugged, and slowly headed up.

**Restricted Area**

# Chapter 9:

# A Waste of Time

As Rebekah and Jonas entered the stairwell in the Cottage Tree, Silver Bear continued on into the forest and up the mountainside. Just as he was reaching the peak, a large brown bear ran up to him.

"Silver Bear, I'm glad I caught you before you went any further," said the out-of-breath bear.

"Bouncer, what urgency brings you to me?"

"Christmas Bear asked me to intercept you on your way to him. Talon told me where you would probably be coming over the mountain. Christmas Bear wants you to go back to Treetop and gather all the bears. He wants you to bring them to Cedar Rest in the morning."

"What's going on?"

"Mr. Nuttybuddy brought news to Christmas Bear of bad wolves coming to Treetop. Mrs. Silver Bear had an encounter with them at the same place you did, and she sent Mr. Nuttybuddy to report it to you and Christmas Bear."

"Is Mrs. Silver Bear alright?" asked Silver Bear—a mix of concern and anger in his voice.

"She's just fine," smiled Bouncer, "but I hear Weed left their meeting with a limp."

Silver Bear grinned, "She never liked that wolf."

"Christmas Bear thanks you for escorting the children to the Summit.

You will reunite with them at Cedar Rest in the morning. I now have to gather the bears in the Summit. I will see you in the morning at Cedar Rest," said Bouncer as he began to head back down his side of the Mountain.

Silver Bear turned to retrace his steps to Treetop. Gathering the Treetop bears would take some time. There was trouble brewing, so he started to run back down the mountain.

The stairway was narrow. It made three complete circles in the trunk to reach the top. The stairs ended at the first level of branches, and the last step brought them out of the trunk facing the tree cottage.

Rebekah and Jonas could now see that the cottage was built on the next branch over from the stairway. The tree trunk webbed the two lower branches together so they could walk from the stairs to the house on a thick bark ledge about three feet wide.

The little house was snow-white with a red roof and brown eaves. There was a big red front door with small Christmas trees on each side of it. There was a green wreath hanging on the red door. The windows on the sides of the house had red shutters with a holly design carved into them. They could see that there were lights on inside.

Rebekah and Jonas made their way to the red door and stopped to listen for sounds of anyone inside. Jonas asked, "Should we knock? I don't hear anybody in there."

"I suppose so," answered Rebekah as she walked up to the door and lightly knocked two times. There was no answer.

Rebekah leaned toward the door and this time knocked harder—3 times. Still there was no answer.

"Silver Bear told us to go into the cottage. He didn't say anything about knocking on the door," reminded Jonas.

"You don't just walk into a house without knocking on the door first," insisted Rebekah.

"Well maybe you do with this one. Besides, you did knock and no one answered. I'm cold. I want to go in."

Without waiting for Rebekah's response, Jonas walked up, placed his hand on the doorknob and turned it slowly and quietly. He opened the door just a crack. They could see a polished wooden floor and they could feel the warmth of the room seeping through the opening.

Rebekah and Jonas stood there for a moment waiting to see if someone would invite them in, but no one did.

Jonas pushed the door open enough to get in and walked inside. He stood a few feet in the doorway and looked around.

"Come on in, Rebekah. There's only one room, it's cozy warm, and there's no one here." Jonas added excitedly, "And my clothes dried the minute I walked through the door!"

That's all Rebekah needed to hear. She had been standing outside wondering about whose house this was and wondering if they should just go inside, but she was freezing as she was doing all that wondering. She walked through the door to join Jonas, and immediately her clothes became dry and soft—just the way they come out of Mama's clothes dryer.

Jonas closed the door behind them. Opposite the door was a fireplace with a low fire burning to keep the house warm—but not too warm. On each side of the fireplace was a small sofa half facing each other and half facing the fire. They noticed some writing on the fireplace mantel and walked closer to read what it said. The inscription read:

*In the beginning, all was bright*
*Working, sowing, reaping*
*Working, knowing, weeping*
*In the beginning came the night*

"I wonder what that means." said Rebekah.

"I don't know," answered Jonas. "Dad says if you can't understand what someone wrote, that person has wasted their time and yours. We probably shouldn't spend a lot of time trying to figure it out."

"It's a poem–that's how poems are."

"And that's why dad says they're a waste of time. If a person has time to think up murky ways to express himself, he has too much time on his hands. And when we spend time reading that stuff, it only encourages more of that silly behavior. Anyway, that's what dad says."

Rebekah let the matter drop and started to stare into the fire.

"I'm a little sleepy," said Jonas. I think I'll rest just a bit until we're told what to do next." Jonas walked to one of the sofas and sat down.

"Me too." Rebekah walked to the other sofa and laid down.

It wasn't long before they were both asleep.

# Chapter 10:

# Hidden Tunnels

"Children...Rebekah...Jonas...it's time to go," said a far-off sounding voice.

Rebekah opened her eyes and saw Jonas stretching and yawning on the sofa opposite hers. "What did you say?"

Jonas looked at her through sleepy eyes. "I didn't say anything. I thought you said something."

"I didn't say anything."

"We must have fallen asleep," said Jonas slowly. "I wonder how long we slept." Jonas sat up quickly. "I hope we didn't mess up our meeting with Christmas Bear! Silver Bear told us we had no time to waste."

"I'm sure someone would have woken us up before we missed our meeting with Christmas Bear," answered Rebekah.

"Someone did wake you up and it's now time to go!" said the same strange voice.

Rebekah and Jonas looked around the room. There was no one there with them. They looked at each other questioningly. Before either of them could say anything, they heard the voice again, "Come on...out the door. Head 'em up — move 'em out!"

Rebekah and Jonas said simultaneously, "Daddy?"

Jonas jumped from the sofa, went to the door, opened it, and stepped outside hoping to see his dad. Rebekah followed him out the door hoping the same thing, but there was no one in sight.

When Jonas turned back toward the house, he was startled by a huge dark figure on the roof.

Rebekah saw Jonas jump and whirled around to see what startled him. There was Talon— perched on top of the cottage chimney. Talon was looking down at them with his cold black eyes.

Rebekah guessed it was Talon who woke them, but she thought it strange that now Talon was using one of Daddy's favorite sayings, *Head 'em up, move 'em out.*

Jonas stared at Talon while walking to Rebekah's side. Talon's face always seemed to have a serious look about it—almost a scowl, and no matter where you were, his eyes always seemed to be on you—piercing, knowing eyes. Jonas mused about how no one in their right mind would buy a stuffed eagle toy for their kid unless they wanted to scare him half to death.

Standing together they both looked up at Talon. Talon just stared back.

Finally Talon spoke. "I never liked the idea of stuffed animals. I thank God you can't easily twist my face into a lifeless, phony smile. Gives the wrong impression of how animals and humans should relate. I'm not some huggy animal you should want to snuggle with at night, so why would you want a stuffed image of me in your bed?"

Rebekah didn't know what he was talking about. Jonas was thinking, *I forgot Talon could hear my thoughts.*

"It's not wise to forget such things!" snapped Talon.

Then Rebekah remembered that Talon heard their thoughts by the exit of the rock passageway in the Summit field. She whispered, "Jonas, are you thinking things that are getting Talon irritated? If you are, stop it!"

"I can't help it. I was just thinking about…"

"Stop thinking about it…whatever it is," admonished Rebekah.

"By the way, Rebekah, your dad is wondering where you are right now," said Talon. "I was thinking of him when I woke you up. That's why I used his words. Did you know that 'Head 'em up, move 'em out' refers to getting cattle moving? I'm amused that he uses the phrase with people."

Talon quickly changed the subject. "It's time for you to be on your way. I want you to walk down the tree branch you are on for as far as you can go and wait for me there."

Rebekah and Jonas looked down the branch. It was a long branch that extended off into the darkness so they couldn't see the end of it.

He repeated himself—a little impatience in his voice, "Walk down the branch as far as you can go and wait for me there!"

"Come on Rebekah, we better just do what he says." Jonas grabbed Rebekah's hand and pulled her in the direction they were to go. They didn't want to leave the cozy cottage, but they headed off down the branch without further hesitation. Jonas didn't like how conversations went with Talon, so he didn't want Rebekah asking…or thinking…any more questions that Talon felt the need to answer.

The branch was as wide as a narrow driveway when they started, but after they had walked a while, it narrowed to about the width of a sidewalk. After a bit more walking, they looked back toward the direction of the cottage, but only saw pine needles and branches. Rebekah and Jonas were a little anxious, but they knew that Silver Bear and Talon were friends. They trusted Silver Bear, so they figured they could trust Talon as well. They continued down the branch.

After just a few more steps, Rebekah and Jonas stopped suddenly. They were at the end of the branch. They were at least thirty feet in the air. They also noticed that the branch ended about one hundred feet from a rock wall.

"Now what," said Jonas?

"Talon told us to wai…" Rebekah never finished her sentence.

As Rebekah was speaking, they heard what sounded like a huge wind coming their direction. Suddenly they were lifted off the branch and were sailing through the air toward the rock ledge.

Rebekah and Jonas didn't even have time to close their eyes. One second they were standing on the branch; the next second they were in mid-air, scared to death. They were headed right for the rock wall and sharply turned left just before hitting it. They sped along the wall just inches above a ledge. They came to an abrupt stop and were set down gently on their bottoms in a corner at the end of the ledge where two rock walls met.

Down came Talon, huge wings open as he touched down in front of them. He then folded his wings and gave them his stoic stare. Rebekah and Jonas, still stunned from their "flight," could only stare back.

"Just doing what needs to be done saves a lot of conversation and whining," instructed Talon.

Luckily, Rebekah and Jonas were still too stunned to think any angry thoughts about Talon scaring them half to death or about his last comment about whining.

"Christmas Bear is waiting for you inside," said Talon.

Rebekah and Jonas looked around them and saw nothing but rock ledge and rock walls.

"Inside where?" asked Jonas

"Follow the tunnel until it ends. Wait there," instructed Talon.

Just then a part of the rock wall started swinging outward. Light seeped out around the outline of a rock door. When the mysterious entrance was completely open, Rebekah and Jonas were sitting in the warm glow of a tunnel's light. They got up and peered into the "hidden" tunnel but could only see as far as the first bend.

"How long should we wai…" Jonas stopped in mid-sentence. As he turned his gaze from the doorway to ask Talon for clarification, there was no Talon. Jonas just caught a glimpse of him as he disappeared into the pines. "Bye, Talon," said Jonas a sarcastically.

Rebekah sighed, "We should be grateful he is helping us. Although I do wish he wouldn't scare me so much. He gives me the shivers every time I see him. He looks like he is always ready to tear somebody's head off."

"Maybe he is," offered Jonas. "Maybe we should be grateful for that, too."

"What do you mean by that?" asked Rebekah

"Oh, I don't know exactly, but remember when we first met Talon? Silver Bear said he or one of his lieutenants meets everyone who comes to the Summit. No one gets in without their permission, remember? Maybe some bad people try to come here without permission. Maybe he fights bad guys."

Rebekah and Jonas sat there and thought about that for a few moments.

"Let's hope we don't need that kind of help," said Rebekah. "I don't want to meet any bad guys. Come on," Rebekah said, getting to her feet. "Let's get to the end of this tunnel."

Rebekah took Jonas' hand and helped him up off the ground. They both took one last look around at the trees, the ledge, and the rock walls, and then they went through the doorway. As soon as they were inside, the rock door began to close back over the entrance. Their initial impulse was to run back to the ledge, but they didn't act on it. Instead, they just watched the door as it thumped shut.

Rebekah and Jonas stood there a while to gather the courage to continue on. It was so quiet in there. It was peaceful and scary at the same time. Slowly, they began to make their way into the mountainside.

**East Summit**

# Chapter 11:

# Scent of Pine

The tunnel was an interesting place. The floor was dirt, but there was no dust. Jonas liked to kick dirt when he walked, and here was no exception—but there was no dust when he did it. There was light in the tunnel—like the light you would get from two or three large candles, but they couldn't figure out where it came from. And the light seemed to follow them; they could see about twenty feet in front and behind them, but it was darkness beyond that. The walls and ceiling were a pinkish white quartz—rough but not sharp or jagged. And the tunnel was getting gradually smaller the farther in they walked. When they first started out, the tunnel was about twelve feet high and maybe eight to ten feet wide. After about thirty minutes of walking, it was about eight feet high and about five feet wide.

"This is a strange place," said Jonas.

"Strange and closing in on us," added Rebekah. "I don't like this," she said as she stretched out both her arms trying to touch the walls. "Look, I can almost touch the ceiling now, too!"

Jonas turned and walked backwards looking at Rebekah jumping up trying to touch the ceiling. "Yeah, it's a lot smaller than when we started, that's for sure."

"Ooooh, no…," sighed Rebekah, stopping and letting her hands fall limply to her sides.

Jonas stopped and turned to look ahead to see what the problem was. Just ahead, the tunnel ended…kind of. The footpath ended into a little cul-de-sac area. In the quartz wall in front of them, about five feet off the ground, was a hole about three feet in diameter right next to the ceiling.

"I don't like the looks of this," said Rebekah.

"What are we supposed to do now?" asked Jonas, staring at the hole in the wall. "Weren't we supposed to wait at the end of the tunnel for….. something?"

"Yes, that's what Talon said," confirmed Rebekah. "We should just wait here."

"I don't think this is the end," said Jonas as he looked at the hole in the wall. "I think we need to keep going."

"I'm not going in that–that's not a tunnel; that's a hole. We'll just wait here. This is the end of the tunnel," insisted Rebekah.

"I don't think this is the end," disagreed Jonas. "We've got to keep going. We certainly can't go back. The rock door closed on us. Even if we could get it open, how would we get off the ledge? We couldn't get back to the tree branch without Talon. Besides, Talon told us Christmas Bear was waiting for us in here. I'm sure Christmas Bear can't come to us through that small hole."

"We're not supposed to go into tunnels. Dad's going to have a fit when he finds out we went into this one by ourselves," said Rebekah. "Going into a small hole in the wall seems to be even worse than what we have already done. What if we get stuck in there?"

"Talon wouldn't have sent us in here to get stuck, and to obey Dad we would have had to stay out of the tunnel altogether. Talon told us we had to go in the tunnel to meet with Christmas Bear, and under the circumstances, I think we did the right thing," reasoned Jonas.

"Ok, Jonas, when we get home, you can explain to Dad that we had to disobey him and go into some tunnels because some big eagle told us to."

Rebekah and Jonas stood in silence for a few moments, not knowing what to do or what else to say. Rebekah looked at the hole and just shook her head. Jonas was looking at the ground thinking.

Finally Jonas asked, "What do you want to do?"

"I don't know what I want to do, but I do know I don't want to go in that hole! Maybe this is where we are supposed to wait," said Rebekah hopefully.

"You can't wait here," said a raspy voice coming from the dark part of the tunnel they just came from.

Rebekah and Jonas both recoiled from the unexpected voice and looked around to see who was doing the talking. They saw no one. They stood very still, trying to hear the slightest sound, but there was dead silence. They looked at each other and then back at the blackness from which they had come.

"Who's there?" asked Jonas as bravely as he could.

"I'm here," said the raspy voice, "and you've got a job to do, so do it."

"Do what?" asked Rebekah. "We were supposed to wait at the end of the tunnel. We're doing that." she said—a little annoyed.

"The tunnel hasn't ended. Get in the smaller tunnel and keep going!" ordered a raspy voice.

"Our Dad told us not to go into tunn...," Jonas was cut off.

"Don't give me that 'Dad' stuff. Your Dad taught you to think, didn't he? Didn't he?" demanded the raspy voice.

Rebekah and Jonas were stunned by the bluntness of the voice.

"Think!" commanded the raspy voice. "You're in Treetop. Silver Bear helped you out of a jam. Silver Bear introduced you to Talon. Talon told you to enter the tunnel. You have to go through this tunnel to get help from Christmas Bear so you can get back home...to your Dad!" said the raspy voice—a little too harshly as far as Rebekah was concerned.

"Look, there's nothing wrong with us wanting to obey our Dad!" said Rebekah. "Maybe we should have told Talon that our Dad said not to go in caves or tunnels without him. Maybe if we had, we could have gone another way to see Christmas Bear."

"Yeah," said Jonas, a little defiantly. "And just because we disobeyed him going into the big tunnel doesn't make it right that we should disobey him more by going into this little tunnel."

"You, look!" said the raspy voice in a very serious tone, "you have to go into that little tunnel to see Christmas Bear. There's no other way out for you. That's not disobeying your Dad, that's making the best decision available to you given the circumstances."

Rebekah and Jonas didn't respond and didn't move any closer to the hole in the wall.

"Ok," said the raspy voice, "you want to obey your Dad? I'm going to provide you with a perfect opportunity."

Rebekah and Jonas didn't like the "I'll show you!" tone in that raspy voice. They remained motionless about fifteen feet from the end of the cul-de-sac. Rebekah and Jonas' hearts were thumping. They knew something was about to happen, but they didn't know what.

Suddenly something flew out of the darkness and landed about ten feet in front of them. It was squirming on the ground…squirming into… into a coil! It had a huge diamond head!

"Rattlesnake!" shouted Rebekah and Jonas in unison as they jumped back and ran until they had their backs against the wall with the hole in the wall just above them. They watched as the rattlesnake uncoiled and started slowly toward them. It stopped about ten feet in front of them and coiled again. It raised its head and opened its mouth to show the scariest fangs you ever wanted to see. Then it rattled. That menacing sound reverberated off the walls making it sound even more dreadful.

The snake had them cornered. Then, in the distance, Rebekah and Jonas heard another rattle…then another…then a bunch all together. More rattlesnakes were coming!

"We gotta get outta this place," whispered Jonas. Jonas guessed the snake had to be at least seven feet long. He was the biggest rattler he had ever seen. It must have been five inches thick in the body. If it hadn't been for the diamond-shaped head and the rattles, Jonas would have thought it was a giant python like the one he once saw at the zoo.

"We've got to go into the hole," whispered Rebekah. "You go first—I'll help you up."

With no argument from Jonas, Rebekah gave him a boost into the small tunnel. It turned out to be exactly like the big tunnel, except it didn't have dirt on the bottom.

Jonas crawled on his knees to make room for Rebekah. The rattlesnake had uncoiled when Jonas entered the hole and was now coming toward Rebekah. Rebekah turned to climb up into the hole but her foot slipped on the quartz wall, and she lost her grip on the small tunnel floor. She slid down the wall and ended up on her rump facing the snake. The snake was right at her feet and was coiling again. Rebekah thought she was done for.

Jonas, hearing Rebekah slip and fall, started scampering backwards in the little tunnel to help her. Unfortunately, he backed out too quickly and fell out of the hole and ended up on his rump right next to Rebekah…and the huge rattlesnake. The snake moved his head back and forth; first in front of Rebekah's face, then in front of Jonas', then by Rebekah's again. His black tongue flicking out as if the snake were licking his lips. Rebekah and Jonas didn't move—not even to look at each other.

"Listen to me," said that raspy voice…coming from the huge snake. "You have nothing to fear from the animals of Treetop if you follow the instructions you are given."

Rebekah and Jonas still didn't move. I suppose they shouldn't have been surprised about a talking snake at this point, but they were. And they were petrified of rattlesnakes!

Just then, three more huge rattlesnakes entered the light and stopped at its edge as if waiting for further instructions.

The rattlesnake with the raspy voice continued, "Get into the small tunnel and continue until it ends just as Talon said. Wait there just like he told you to do. We can't help you very much if you don't follow instructions. And you won't follow our instructions very well if you don't have trust."

"It's hard to be trusting in a strange place where every experience we've had so far has been scary or unbelievable. We've had wolves try to get us, and we've been talking to animals all day that aren't supposed to talk," said Rebekah.

"Excuse me for saying this, but it seems extra hard to trust rattlesnakes," said Jonas apologetically as he glanced from the big snake to the ones at the edge of the light.

"I never said anything about trusting me," corrected the rattlesnake. "When you are lost in a strange place where things don't seem to be as they should—that's where you need trust the most. You must know Him or you couldn't be here."

Rebekah and Jonas sat there with surprised looks on their faces.

"Him being God, of course," the snake clarified.

Rebekah and Jonas began to relax a bit. They were a little embarrassed that they had to be reminded by a rattlesnake to trust God in all circumstances—especially difficult ones.

Rebekah started to move to get up, then stopped reflexively because of the rattlesnake at her feet. The rattlesnake understood exactly what Rebekah was thinking.

"You may get up, Rebekah. I won't strike at you." There was a hint—just a hint—of kindness in that raspy voice.

As Rebekah slowly stood up, she noticed the faint scent of pine in the tunnel. When Jonas stood, he noticed it, too.

"I smell pine," whispered Jonas.

"I smell it, too, but it's odd because we're in a tunnel. How did the scent get in here all of a sudden?" whispered Rebekah.

"Pine is such a pleasant scent, don't you think?" asked the rattlesnake. "I prefer it above all others."

"We like the smell, too," answered Jonas, "but I was surprised to smell it in this tunnel. There are no pine trees here."

"Could we be close to the end of the tunnel?" asked Rebekah hopefully. "Are we close to an opening where we will be out in the trees again?"

The rattlesnake ignored her questions and said, "Pine is the most significant scent in Treetop. Without the pine scent, Treetop wouldn't exist as it does."

"But we didn't smell pine when we first came into the tunnel and we didn't notice it when we first came to this dead end. Why do we smell it now?" Then Jonas repeated Rebekah's question, "Are we close to an opening to the forest?"

"No, that's not it. It's not the trees—at least it's not the trees in here. It's us—my associates and I—that's who you smell. All the animals in Treetop have the pine scent...even rattlesnakes."

"Rattlesnakes smell like pine trees?" said Rebekah in astonishment.

"We noticed the pine scent on Silver Bear's fur. He said Christmas Bear's fur smells like pine—just like the Christmas Bear in our Daddy's story. So how come you all have a pine scent?" asked Jonas.

"It's a security measure. It's how we tell who belongs here and who doesn't. Not just any animal is allowed in Treetop. You must have the scent, or you will be cast out—or killed."

"A security measure? How come you need such a security measure in Treetop?" asked Jonas

"Treetop is a very special place. Special places need to be protected from those who think there is nothing more special than themselves. Otherwise, the special places will be ruined. All of us in Treetop have a responsibility to see that our borders are not breached by enemies. We also must make sure we do not associate with or share information with enemies who would harm us or spoil Treetop. Our unique scent is a gift from God that helps us discern the good from the bad."

"Who are your enemies," asked Jonas with interest, "and why do they want to harm you and spoil Treetop? And what do you mean by 'spoil' Treetop?

"Those are great questions, Jonas, and they will be answered—but not by me. We've talked too long already. You must get going. Christmas Bear is waiting for you, but he can't wait too much longer. He has to begin his rounds soon—into the small tunnel with the both of you."

Rebekah felt much better about going into the hole now. She turned to give Jonas a boost into the small tunnel, but not so much in a rush this time. Jonas put his foot in Rebekah's clasped hands, grabbed the base of the small tunnel and paused to look back at the snake.

"Do you have a name?"

"My name is Striker."

Rebekah smiled, "We should have guessed."

"By the way, you're not really disobeying your father by going into a small tunnel. You are not going in there by choice—you don't have a choice. Didn't he also tell you to keep away from rattlesnakes?" Striker said with a chuckle. "You can't do both things here. You can take the tunnel with a clear conscience."

Rebekah and Jonas thought they heard muffled laughter coming from the other snakes in the tunnel.

"Thank you, Striker," said Jonas.

Rebekah gave Jonas the boost up, and he again was in the small tunnel. Rebekah turned back to Striker and said, "Thank you for watching over us. Thank you for reminding us to trust God in all circumstances, especially the tough ones. We'll try not to forget that again." Rebekah smiled at Striker, turned, grabbed the bottom of the small tunnel with both hands, pulled herself up, and disappeared into the hole in the wall.

**"We gotta get outta this place."**

# Chapter 12:

# Christmas Bear

About thirty-five wolves were scattered on the rocks of the hilltop as Skull approached the meeting area. The growling and yipping of his mid-ranked followers slowly quieted as he climbed up on his speaking rock. He looked out at them for a few moments. *What a bunch of incompetent misfits* he thought. *How am I going to challenge Treetop with troops like these?* Skull then announced, "Humans have entered Treetop." Most of the wolves had already heard the news, but murmuring spread throughout the group anyway.

"Our attempt at preventing that from happening failed," reported Skull as he glared at Weed. Weed tried to glare back, but soon lost his nerve and looked away from Skull. "We must now prevent them from leaving Treetop. If they are allowed to return home, our lives could be in jeopardy."

"Why didn't we have more wolves watching the borders to keep the humans out to begin with?" came a shout from one of the wolves.

Skull bristled at the question – he hated to be second-guessed – but he managed to keep his temper and replied, "First, we didn't know when the humans would return. Secondly, more of us on the borders would have increased the risk of being detected and of arousing suspicion. We didn't want to alert the Treetoppers of our border watch." Then Skull's voice became louder and more menacing, "You all would have known that if more of you would have attended my strategy meetings!" Skull glared at the crowd waiting for more questions. No one risked asking another.

Skull continued, "If we can keep the Treetoppers preoccupied with the safety of the humans, they will have less time to focus on us."

"What makes you think our efforts can change anything?" shouted out one of the younger, less cautious wolves.

Skull began a deep growl and started toward the young upstart. Dameon stepped in front of Skull as he replied to the young wolf, "It would be foolish not to try to do something," said Dameon." "Waiting for our enemies to move first will give them the advantage. Like Skull said, we must do what we can to keep them preoccupied with the humans." Then Dameon whispered to Skull, "Fighting amongst ourselves now is not going to help us."

The hair on Skull's back flattened. He stopped his advance on the younger wolf and said to the group, "I need each of you to summon as many warriors as you can for a battle planning meeting later this evening. Go through your areas and tell everyone we will be leaving tonight. We must be at Treetop by morning. Move!" shouted Skull.

The wolves left the hill to gather an army. Soon the meeting area was deserted except for Skull and Dameon.

Skull said to Dameon, "You will instruct the troops at tonight's meeting. Lead them to Treetop. Get there before morning. I will be leaving for Treetop immediately. Send Stickers and Weed to me right away!"

Skull walked off without saying another word and went back to lying on the rock that overlooked the weed field.

Dameon went to find Stickers and Weed. He also had to prepare for the evening meeting and the march on Treetop.

As the wolves dispersed from the hill, a lone eagle launched off a nearby tree and quietly flew off to the east.

The small tunnel had a slight incline to it, and it curved to the left so Jonas could not see more than a few yards ahead of him. After crawling a little ways, the tunnel widened enough for Rebekah to crawl alongside Jonas.

"I'm glad this got wider," said Rebekah. "I didn't like being so closed in."

"Me, too" said Jonas, "I just hope we don't have to crawl too much farther. This hard rock hurts my knees."

In just a few minutes, the little tunnel straightened out and they could see it ended a little ways ahead. They could also see that a tree branch partially blocked the exit hole. Beyond the branch, they saw a fire in a fireplace. They crawled to within a few feet of the exit and stopped to listen. They only heard the crackling of the fire.

"Let's go check it out," whispered Rebekah. "This must be where we'll meet Christmas Bear."

Rebekah and Jonas poked their heads out of the tunnel and peered into the room. It was about the size of their mom and dad's bedroom. There was a Christmas tree to their left decorated with red berries and little figures of all kinds of animals. It was a live tree, growing up through the floor. The fireplace was in the wall opposite them. There was a rug in the center of the room that reached from the edge of the tree to the hearth of the fireplace. There was a large door to their right with windows on each side of it. No one was in the room.

Jonas was the first to crawl out of the tunnel and onto the carpet. It was very thick and soft. Rebekah followed him out and they both sat down in front of the tree—facing the fireplace.

"I suppose we should just wait here," said Rebekah. "Talon told us to go to the end of the tunnel and wait."

"Yep," said Jonas, "and this is a pretty nice place to wait if you ask me."

Rebekah glanced back at the tree and noticed the ornaments once again. They were little carved figures of bears, wolves, mountain lions, wolverines, bobcats, porcupines, skunks, squirrels, chipmunks, otters, beavers, rabbits, birds, horses, deer, elk, moose, and snakes.

"Snakes?" muttered Rebekah, "Who would put snakes on their Christmas tree?"

Jonas' attention was drawn to the tree. "Snakes where?"

"Right there," she pointed to the bottom center of the tree.

"Christmas Bear must like snakes. Then Jonas noticed an ornament tucked way back near the trunk of the tree. It was a little house. He crawled over to the tree and stuck his head in the branches to get a closer look at the house. It looked very similar to the tree cottage they had been in a short time ago. There was an ornament of two figures, a little boy and girl, hanging next to it.

"Hey, look at this! A little house like the one we were in back in the forest with two kids next to it." Jonas quickly scanned the tree. "It looks like they are the only ornaments that aren't of animals."

Rebekah got to her feet and walked around the tree. Sure enough, all the other ornaments were likenesses of animals.

Rebekah and Jonas were distracted from their scrutiny of the tree by the sound of voices outside. Then someone knocked on the door twice. After a brief pause, the door slowly opened. There in the doorway was the biggest white bear Rebekah and Jonas ever saw. It was showing some of its teeth, but by now Rebekah and Jonas had learned what a bear grin looked like. Without saying a word, the huge bear squeezed through the doorway and laid down on the carpet in front of them. After him, a huge silver grey wolf—very similar in color to Silver Bear—walked through the doorway, turned, pushed the door shut, and then sat down in front of the door without making a sound. The room filled with the scent of pine.

The bear was still grinning at Rebekah and Jonas. "You don't know how blessed it is to finally meet you. I'm Christmas Bear, and he," nodding to the big wolf at the door, "is Stalker."

The wolf didn't move or show any sign of acknowledging Rebekah or Jonas. He just stared at them with his gray/black eyes. His demeanor reminded them of Talon.

"So, I understand you don't know how to get back home. I think I can help you with that." Christmas Bear said encouragingly. "You've been with me on my rounds before…do you remember?" The bear's eyes twinkled as he smiled at them. "In your Dad's story…you got lost in the woods…you helped with my rounds and I brought you home. Remember?"

"Ahhh…well….that story was about Jabekah and Ronas, two puppies….," began Rebekah.

Christmas Bear let out a laugh, "Yes, yes…Jabekah and Ronas. Very clever play on your names, but you were there just the same, weren't you?"

"That was just a story," said Jonas cautiously.

"Yes, it was a story," confirmed Christmas Bear, "but it was a true story—it just hadn't happened yet. Your dad's story was to help prepare you for your visit here so you wouldn't be so afraid when you arrived."

"You mean our daddy knew he was telling us a story that was going to come true? He knew we were going to come here one day?" asked Rebekah.

"No, I don't think he knew that. He had what I call hidden inspiration. He was prompted by God to tell you a story that would later help you feel less frightened when it actually happened to you. God does that sometimes."

"This is really strange," said Jonas. "Dad's story…us being here now. How did we get here? Why did we come? What are we supposed to do?"

"Ah, that's what I like, Jonas, a man who wants to get right to the point. And the point is, we have been waiting for you two for a long time. I am going to explain the whole thing to you before we start on my rounds."

They were interrupted by a single knock on the door, and Stalker got up out of the way as the door seemed to open by itself. Then Rebekah and Jonas saw the strangest thing—two chipmunks pulling a tiny sleigh holding two steaming cups of something. The chipmunks pulled the sleigh on the carpet between Christmas Bear and the children. They then slipped their harnesses and scampered up into the Christmas tree.

"Thank you, Zeek and Jitter—perfect timing."

Christmas Bear looked at Rebekah and Jonas, smiled and said, "Enjoy your cocoa while we chat a bit."

**Perfect Timing**

# Chapter 13:

# A History Lesson

T he hot cocoa was the best they had ever tasted. It was creamy and very chocolaty and had something in it that gave it a kind of pleasant perfumey smell. It was topped with a mountain of whipped cream. The cups looked like pine cones. It was the perfect Christmas Eve drink.

"Have you gotten used to talking animals yet?" asked Christmas Bear cheerfully. "Silver Bear tells me you were quite surprised when he spoke to you. And then there was Mr. Nuttybuddy, and Mrs. Silver Bear, and Talon, and Striker, and me…and Stalker, too, when he wants to."

Rebekah and Jonas couldn't help but smile because of Christmas Bear's joyful nature, but it was still odd to them that these animals talked.

"Animals don't talk where we come from," offered Jonas

"And why don't they, do you suppose?" asked Christmas Bear

"Well, they don't talk because….animals don't talk," answered Jonas.

"They don't?" ask Christmas Bear joking with Jonas. "Then how come this big white bear is talking to you?"

"They talk in Treetop, but not where we live," said Rebekah, coming to Jonas' defense.

"And why do you think that is?"

There was a long pause, and then Rebekah replied, "We don't know."

"Have you ever heard about animals talking to people before?"

Rebekah and Jonas thought for a minute.

"In cartoons and movies?" guessed Jonas.

"Good answer, Jonas!" said Christmas Bear, "but that's pretend. Have you ever heard about real animals talking to real people?"

There was a longer pause this time as Rebekah and Jonas pondered Christmas Bear's question.

"Balaam's donkey talked to Balaam when he was being mean," said Rebekah, "but that was a long time ago in the Bible."

"And the snake! The snake talked to Eve in the Garden of Eden. That's in the Bible, too," added Jonas.

"So you see," said Christmas Bear, "there have been times and places where animals and people have talked with each other."

"But those were miracles in the Bible," said Rebekah. "Animals didn't always talk with people."

"You are partially right," said Christmas Bear encouragingly. "Balaam's donkey talking to Balaam in a fallen, sinful world was a miracle. But the snake—he talked to Eve before The Fall. Before The Fall, that was not a miracle—that's just how it was."

Rebekah and Jonas hadn't given much thought to animals speaking to people before Eve was deceived by the snake in the Garden of Eden.

Christmas Bear continued, "Do you think Eve could have been so easily fooled by a talking snake if she had never heard a snake talk before? And she talked back to the snake as if it were a natural thing to do, remember?"

"That's how the story goes," said Rebekah.

"Oh, Rebekah, it's more than just a story. It's History. It happened just like it says in the Bible. In the garden, God allowed the animals to talk to Adam and Eve—just like you and I are talking right now. It was such a beautiful time..." Christmas Bear paused in mid-sentence. For a few moments, he seemed to be far off in thought as he stared past them at the Christmas tree.

"The way you tell it," said Jonas, "makes me feel like you were there."

Christmas Bear looked at Jonas—and then to Rebekah. "I was. I am. You are now."

"You were in the Garden of Eden!" exclaimed Rebekah. "How could that be? That was thousands of years ago! How could that be?"

"I was in the Garden, and I am in the Garden. I never left it. And now, by God's mercy, you have come to the Garden to give us the message that we have been waiting for—as you said, Rebekah—for thousands of years.

Rebekah and Jonas looked at each other blankly. Christmas Bear had been waiting all these years for a message from them, and they had nothing to tell him. If God sent them here, why didn't He tell them what the message was that they were supposed to deliver? When they looked back at Christmas Bear, he could tell they were concerned about something.

"What's the matter with you two?" he asked kindly.

"Christmas Bear, we don't have a message to give you," said Jonas sadly.

"Nobody told us to give you one," added Rebekah apologetically. "We don't know what to say to you."

Christmas Bear smiled. "You don't have to say anything. You ARE the message."

Rebekah and Jonas looked at each other again, this time with puzzled looks.

"God sent you here to accomplish a very important part of his plan. We are grateful that you have come to us. You should try to enjoy your Treetop experience as much as you can while He has you here." advised Christmas Bear.

"We don't understand any of this," said Rebekah. "Please don't think us ungrateful for the protection and welcome we have received here, but we just want to get home. Treetop is the most beautiful place I have ever seen, but we miss our family. Even though God sent us to you, we still feel lost— and that is a little scary. This is all so confusing."

"Our mom and dad have to be worried sick about us by this time," added Jonas.

"Oh, don't worry about your folks. I know it seems like you have been here a long time, but only a few minutes have passed where you came from."

"So you do know where we came from?" asked Rebekah hopefully.

"Yes, I know where you came from."

"Then you know where our house is? You can get us home?" asked Jonas excitedly.

"I will help you find your home, but to do so, you will have to follow our directions precisely—just like you have been doing." Christmas Bear's tone became very serious, "I warn you now that there are those who will try to stop you from getting back to your Bell Rock Road."

Rebekah and Jonas looked at Christmas Bear with concern. *Who would want to keep us from getting back home?*

Christmas Bear replied, "The same bunch of thugs, along with others like them, that gave you trouble at the rock cave. They did not want you entering Treetop, and now that you are here—they don't want you to leave."

Rebekah and Jonas glanced at each other. Jonas spoke, "We don't understand."

"Your confusion and concerns about all this are understandable. Let me explain some things to help you feel more comfortable with your situation," offered Christmas Bear.

Rebekah and Jonas sipped on their cocoa as Christmas Bear told them an incredible story.

"Long ago, in the beginning, God made everything—and he made everything perfectly. On the fifth and sixth days, He created animals and man. He created animals first, and then he created Adam and Eve. You both know history this far, but what you don't know is that after a time, some of the animals began to resent the creation of man. This was the work of Lucifer, of course. He was preparing to deceive Eve, and his plan included stirring up the animals to help him do it."

"Why did all the animals resent Adam and Eve?" asked Jonas.

"And who is Lucifer?" asked Rebekah.

"Only some of the animals had this resentment," corrected Christmas Bear. "Some of us remained true to God and did not fall for Lucifer's schemes, but others were weak."

There were a few moments of silence before Christmas Bear continued. Rebekah and Jonas could tell this story made him sad.

"Lucifer is better known to you as Satan—or the devil, Rebekah. He is a very bad angel. Lucifer began to suggest to the animals that they had had a better relationship with God before Adam was created. He reminded them that before Adam, they walked and talked with God more freely. He emphasized the fact that animals were created before Adam, and argued persuasively that they, therefore, shouldn't have to serve or obey Adam. Some prideful animals wanted to believe his lies."

"Why was Lucifer trying to make the animals dislike Adam," asked Rebekah.

"Lucifer hated Adam for the attention and authority God was giving to him. His envy was so great that he devised a plan to entice Eve to disobey God's law. Lucifer knew that disobedience to the law would cause Adam and Eve to be kicked out of the Garden. He didn't want them enjoying the Garden that he thought should have been his to enjoy and control. With Adam and Eve out of the way, Lucifer believed he would increase in influence and status."

"Why did Lucifer use a snake?" asked Jonas. "Everybody knows most girls don't like snakes."

"Very good question, Jonas," said Christmas Bear, "but you must try to see things as they were in the Garden in the beginning. Lucifer knew that Adam and Eve didn't normally meet with angels, so they would be wary of an angel who approached them to suggest something contrary to the law God had given to them. So instead of approaching Eve himself, he used a snake for his deception. Back then animals talked to Adam and Eve on a regular basis. The relationship between Adam and all the animals was perfect. Remember, Adam was given the task of naming all the animals, so Adam and Eve and the animals became very close."

"And Eve loved snakes," continued Christmas Bear. "I wouldn't go so far as to say they were her favorite animal, but she was fascinated with how God had made them and thought they were very beautiful. I never saw Eve without a snake in her presence."

Rebekah was fascinated by what she was hearing. *Christmas Bear knew Eve! He really was in the Garden of Eden!*

Jonas was having similar thoughts: *How could this bear have been in the Garden of Eden, know Eve, and still be alive today?*

Christmas Bear smiled at them. "I know it's hard for you to believe what I just told you, but it's true. I knew both Adam and Eve, and as I told you before, I am in the Garden of Eden—present tense. It's not just a place I have been. I'm still here."

Rebekah looked back at Christmas Bear. "You can hear our thoughts, too!"

"Yes," said Christmas Bear, "I can. Talon can, as you have already found out. Striker and Stalker can do it, too."

Rebekah and Jonas looked at Stalker by the door. He was watching them—staring at them. He looked scary, and they now knew he knew that they were thinking that.

"Don't be concerned about Stalker. He's your ally, even if you can't tell by looking at him.

"Now, let's get back to your last question, Jonas. As I was saying, Eve loved snakes—and Lucifer knew it. Lucifer found a snake that believed his lies and that had become resentful of Adam and Eve. He told the snake that the only way the animals could get back their first place position with God was to make Adam and Eve sin. The snake agreed to cooperate with Lucifer.

"Eve was deceived by Lucifer using an animal she loved and trusted. I'm not making excuses for her foolishness, but I think you can now understand a little better why her guard was down.

"After Adam and Eve sinned, a cloud of fear swept over the Garden. I can remember that day like it was yesterday," said Christmas Bear as he stared off into the Christmas tree again. It looked as if he was reliving that day all over again, and he was completely lost in his thoughts.

Rebekah and Jonas sat silently and waited for Christmas Bear to come back to them. They glanced over at Stalker, and they noticed a slight change in him. He was still by the door, but his head was down and he was staring at the floor. His face was no longer like stone; it looked sad—very sad. He was reliving that day, too.

"I was afraid…we were afraid…all of us were afraid," continued Christmas Bear–still staring into the tree. "We were afraid, but we didn't know what fear was—this feeling was completely new to us. Then our sense of smell and hearing became magnified many times over. We heard things we couldn't see, smelled things we couldn't see, ran from things we couldn't see, and could no longer speak to anyone. We didn't know why these things were happening or why we felt so—so horrible. It was the worst of days."

Christmas Bear paused in His story. Rebekah and Jonas glanced over at Stalker again. He had regained his composure—his expression was as cold and fearsome as ever. Christmas Bear shifted his position, and he looked back at the children.

"God's wrath can be severe," he warned. "You don't ever want to provoke Him to wrath, but Adam, Eve, Lucifer, and the snake did just that. As a consequence, sin and fear came into existence. The bliss of the Garden had been ruined.

"However, the Lord is merciful. The loyal animals didn't have to suffer the consequences of sin for long. Those who had remained true to Him were restored. He took away those new fears that came with sin and gave us back our ability to speak. As a reward for our loyalty, He allowed us to keep our heightened senses. It was also the day He gave us our distinctive pine scent. He gave us the scent so we could easily distinguish the loyal animals from the rebels. He then told us to round up all the animals without the pine scent and bring them to the north entrance to the Garden.

"It was a sad sight," Christmas Bear continued. "Animals we fellow-shipped with and considered our friends the day before were angry, howling, cringing, snarling, pitiful creatures. We herded them to the north entrance. They were forced to huddle together on one side of the north garden path. We stood on the other side of the path—lined up like a platoon of soldiers—facing them. There were angels with swords around the rebellious animals and one angel with a flaming sword at the north entrance. Adam and Eve had to walk down that path between us to leave the Garden. Their heads were bowed down; they were so ashamed. They never looked at any of us as they walked slowly past. They were crying. No words were exchanged—no good byes—nothing. They walked out, and we haven't seen a human since—until now.

"The Lord then ordered the rebellious animals herded to the north border of the Garden to the top of our highest mountain. You saw it on your way up to the Summit when you were in the climbing tunnel. We escorted them to the peak of what was Summit Mountain—where the deception had taken place. There He banished the rebellious animals to the place we call Rustcoat.

"When the Lord was finished passing judgment, the loyal animals were then ordered by an archangel to leave the area quickly. We hurried back to a meadow a few thousand feet below the mountain top. More angels were waiting for us there and told us to turn, look toward Summit Mountain, and stand quietly until told to do otherwise. Then it began."

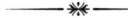

**"…the worst of days."**

# Chapter 14:

# Wrath

Rebekah and Jonas were captivated by Christmas Bear's account of The Fall. Jonas had often wondered how Eve could have been so stupid as to be deceived by a talking snake. Now it made some sense. Rebekah often wondered about The Fall, too, but was a little more gracious in her thinking about Eve. Neither of them had ever bothered to take the time to try to think it through.

Christmas Bear interrupted their thoughts, "You shouldn't be too hard on yourselves for not having a reasonable understanding of The Fall. Most of your preachers haven't "thought it through" well enough to understand it, let alone attempt to explain it to their congregations. The creation account in the Bible is history – not just a story. Most preachers say they believe the Bible is God's inerrant word, yet they seldom act like it. The Bible teaches many things that are foolishness to those who are not elect. Preachers who fear people more than they fear God misrepresent His story to allow their followers to be comfortable in their sins. These false teachers would rather be popular in their world than true to God's word. Their faith is weak, if it exists at all, and they don't want to be bound by God's laws because it restricts their so-called 'freedom.' Freedom to sin is the freedom they preach. It's no wonder most people have an irrelevant faith. These 'spiritual' leaders preach half the gospel – which is no gospel at all. They are a despicable bunch of pandering cowards."

Christmas Bear gave a long sigh, composed himself, and paused to smile at Rebekah and Jonas. "Anyway, before I continued with my history lesson, I wanted to address any concerns you have about not 'thinking through' The Fall." explained Christmas Bear'

"But we didn't express any concerns," said Jonas, but as soon as he said it, he remembered that Christmas Bear could hear their thoughts.

"Wow," said Jonas, "You gotta be careful what you think around here."

"Jonas, you should be careful about what you think wherever you are. We're not the ones you should be worried about hearing your thoughts," advised Christmas Bear.

Now then, where was I in the story?"

"The last thing you said was, "Then it began…" answered Rebekah

"Oh, yes! 'Then it began…'…the ground began to shake under our feet. We were startled—but none of us moved. The ground rumbled, and it felt like waves moving under us toward the peak. The shaking became more violent. The ground split open and a huge chasm separated Summit Mountain from the rest of the Garden. The mountain began to sink into the chasm. We could see the rebel animals huddled in fear. Huge stones rolled down the mountainside—mowing down trees in their paths. Then big chunks of the mountainside gave way and fell into the chasm. Then lightning struck the mountain and the remaining trees caught fire." Christmas Bear paused just long enough for Jonas to get in a question.

"Christmas Bear, you said we saw this mountain—Summit Mountain—as we were climbing to this Summit in the climbing tunnel. What mountain was it? I don't remember seeing it."

"I can understand how you wouldn't recognize it. The original Summit Mountain in the Garden was 14,700 feet high. Silver Bear pointed it out to you as Mt. Ugga. It now stands at 7700 feet, and as you saw, nothing beautiful grows on it. It is nothing but a heap of weeds, broken rock and barren ground. It crumbled down 7000 feet the day of the earthquake. The faithful animals stood to watch the Lord's judgment on the rebel animals at the same place you left the climbing tunnel and first met Talon.

"When the shaking stopped, two-thirds of the rebel animals had perished in the landslides and fires. The remaining third were to populate Rustcoat with animals that were to coexist with sinful man. They and their offspring were not to serve man willingly, and sinful man would kill or tame them as his needs required. It's a horrible existence for them, but sometimes justice requires such unpleasantness." Christmas Bear paused again and this time Rebekah had a question.

"So the animals that tried to get us when we first arrived in Treetop are the offspring of the rebel animals that were kicked out of the Garden?"

"Some are offspring, and some are the original trouble makers. The offspring of the rebels die, but the rebels themselves were shown no such mercy. Three of the wolves that attacked you earlier this evening; Dameon, Stickers, and Weed, were among the original Rebels. The other two were newcomers. Silver Bear sensed trouble when he saw those three back in Treetop. When he saw that they were after you, he knew something significant was up and that I needed to be informed of it."

"Why were they trying to keep Jonas and me out of Treetop?" asked Rebekah.

"To delay their final judgement," answered Christmas Bear.

"Their final judgment?" asked Jonas.

"During the destruction of Summit Mountain, most of the animals turned away because they could not watch it, even though they were instructed to do so. Talon, Stalker, Striker, and I were the only ones who kept our eyes on the destruction the entire time. To reward us, God revealed a little of His future plans to the four of us. He told us that the rebels' final judgment would come when he allowed man back into the Garden. We were to watch for that sign to be given to us. God also told us he would reveal a hint of this plan to Skull so he would have no peace in Rustcoat. Knowledge given to evil ones can be very unsettling for them because they lack wisdom."

"So that's why you said we are the message," concluded Jonas. "We are the first people to enter the Garden since The Fall."

"Right, and what better representatives for man than children with the child-like faith and humility that God requires for sanctification. God is perfect. You can see it in everything he does."

"So if this is all part of God's plan, why do the rebel animals resist it?" asked Rebekah.

"The rebels still don't understand God's sovereignty. They thought they could thwart God's plan by keeping man from entering the Garden again. They have been incessantly watching our borders for thousands of years because of that misguided belief. But that's what sin does—it distracts you from useful work and mires you in useless, meaningless worry and activity that leads only to frustration and failure."

"I wonder why He picked Jonas and me," asked Rebekah.

"God has assignments for each of us," answered Christmas Bear. "We may not know why we were chosen to do what we do, to experience what we experience, to suffer what we suffer—but God knows. He has a perfect plan and always selects the perfect person at the perfect time for the perfect task. There is comfort in knowing that, and that is really all we have to know about it. Isn't that right?"

Rebekah and Jonas agreed that it was very comforting to know that God has all things worked out for good, but they still had more questions about how they fit in God's plan in Treetop.

"You said the rebellious animals would suffer a final judgment when we... I mean 'when man'... returned to the Garden," said Rebekah. "What is their final judgment?"

"Death. They will be hunted down and killed for their disobedience. God forced them to suffer a miserable life in Rustcoat for a time, but that time will soon be coming to an end."

"Who is going to hunt them down and kill them?" asked Jonas.

"The Treetop warriors will do that," answered Christmas Bear.

"Treetop warriors!" Jonas said excitedly. "You have warriors?"

Christmas Bear smiled at Jonas. "We have enough to do God's work."

"When will this warfare take place?" asked Rebekah.

"It begins tomorrow. After you are safely back home, we will begin to seek and destroy rebel animals in all of Rustcoat —first in your home area and then spreading out over the whole earth."

"So that's why the rebels will try to stop us from leaving Treetop— because once we're home you go after them?" asked Jonas.

"Yes. We can't begin our search and destroy missions until you are safely back home. We can't start the second phase of our assignment until we have completed the first one successfully."

"They're going to try to kill us, aren't they?" sighed Rebekah. "They must be really angry with us for being this message to you."

"They wouldn't dare kill you," answered Christmas Bear. "Their survival depends on keeping our warriors occupied with your safety. They will try to keep you in Treetop, or they may try to capture you and hide you somewhere. These two strategies, if successful, would delay the search and destroy missions."

"Can they keep us here?" asked Rebekah. "Could they capture us?"

"I can only say that they will try. I can tell you that we will do everything we can to get you home. The rest is up to the Lord. We must trust him with the outcome."

Jonas had another question. "Christmas Bear, are all the animals not in Treetop considered Rebel animals?"

"Not all of them are considered rebels, but a good many animals follow the rebel leaders."

"Then not all the animals on earth have to be killed?" asked Jonas.

"Not all of them." answered Christmas Bear. "We are primarily after the rebels who were kicked out of Eden for following Lucifer. However, the animals who have supported and followed these rebels will also be eliminated."

"How will this purge change things for God's people?" was Jonas' final question.

"Eliminating some of the evil in a place always makes it a better place, but exactly how different things will be hasn't been made known to me. What I do know is that God knows what he is doing, and the wise thing for us to do is to follow his instructions and leave the results to him."

Christmas Bear then turned to Stalker, "Stalker, I believe it's time we started the rounds. Would you please go get my sack? We'll wait for you at the beginning of Sprucewalk."

"Zeek?" Christmas Bear said scanning the Christmas tree behind the children.

"Zeek scampered to the edge of a branch near the top of the tree. "You called, sir?" Zeek squeaked.

"I would like you to find Mr. Nuttybuddy. I want you, Jitter and Mr. Nuttybuddy to gather the others for a meeting at Cedar Rest. I will come there with the Children after my rounds are completed.

"Will do," said Zeek. Zeek muttered something to Jitter who was still hidden in the Christmas tree. Stalker opened the door, and Zeek scampered off to do as he was asked. Jitter climbed down the tree, smiled and waved at Rebekah and Jonas, and then disappeared into the little tunnel from which Rebekah and Jonas had entered the room.

Rebekah and Jonas followed Christmas Bear out of the Christmas tree room and into the cold night. There was a huge mountain behind them and a pine forest all around them. The ground was white with snow and the whole place glowed from the light of a huge moon.

They saw Zeek talking with Talon some distance away. They watched as another eagle swooped into the conversation. Zeek then climbed on the other eagle's back and the eagle flew off toward the mountain behind them. Talon stared at them for a moment and then flew off in the opposite direction.

"Let's go," said Christmas Bear. "It will take us just a few minutes to get to the beginning of Sprucewalk."

Rebekah and Jonas followed Christmas Bear off into the trees.

# Chapter 15:

# The Mustering

J itter made his way to the end of the small tunnel and peered down into the larger tunnel. He saw a group of snakes in the cul-de-sac huddled in conversation.

"Striker!" said Jitter. "I'm glad you're still here. Christmas Bear sent me to ask for your help. He wants the soldiers gathered at Cedar Rest for a meeting after he completes his rounds with the children. Can you and your lieutenants notify the rest of the snakes of the meeting? If you could also ask Grizzle to have his wolverines attend, that would be a great help."

"Will do, and if you like, we'll notify Whiskers, too." offered Striker. "He's in Grizzle's area, and he can get the message to the rest of his cougars."

"That would be great!" said Jitter. "If you'll do that, I'll head down the mountain to help Zeek with the others. See you at Cedar Rest."

Jitter turned and disappeared back up the small tunnel.

"It looks like the showdown has finally come," said Striker to the three snakes—still looking at the small tunnel where Jitter had appeared. He turned his gaze back to the group of snakes. "Vennie, I need you to spread the word to the snakes in the Summit. Winder, Slither, I would like you to go down the mountain and gather everyone there. I'll notify Whiskers and Grizzle on my way to Cedar Rest. We better get going."

Winder and Slither took off down the tunnel. Striker and Vennie disappeared into cracks in the tunnel wall.

The huge eagle swooped down under an Aspen tree and landed right next to Mr. Nuttybuddy. Mr. Nuttybuddy was so surprised that he jumped sideways from the eagle and hit his head on the Aspen next to him. He fell on his back in a daze.

Zeek giggled as Mr. Nuttybuddy shook himself upright and glared at Zeek and the eagle.

"Bomber," cried Mr. Nuttybuddy, "you scared the wits out of me! And Zeek, you stop that giggling at once. There's just no respect for elders around here anymore!"

"I'm sorry Mr. Nuttybuddy. We didn't mean to scare you," apologized Zeek—trying to muffle another giggle. "Bomber was flying over and saw you under the tree at the last minute and quickly turned to make his landing."

Mr. Nuttybuddy scowled at Zeek and Bomber. "A squirrel can have a heart attack, you know!" "You could have circled around and flown up to me from the front, Bomber…that's what you should have done. There was no call to…"

"Zeek has some news for you, Mr. Nuttybuddy," Bomber said emotionlessly. "I suggest you calm down and listen to what he has to tell you."

"See here, Bomber. Don't you tell me to calm down when you just scared me half to death. I think you owe me an…."

Bomber interrupted Mr. Nuttybuddy again. "The message is from Christmas Bear, and it is urgent," said Bomber as he put his face right up to Mr. Nuttybuddy's. "Stop complaining and listen."

Bomber and Mr. Nuttybuddy glared at each other for a few moments, but an eagle's glare is much scarier than a squirrel's, so Mr. Nuttybuddy backed down and turned to Zeek.

"What's the message from Christmas Bear?" asked Mr. Nuttybuddy—trying to take the edge off his voice.

"Christmas Bear wants you and me to gather the Treetoppers in the Circle for a meeting at Cedar Rest. As soon as he finishes his rounds with the Children, he will be bringing them there for the meeting," squeaked Zeek.

"The children! I knew they were trouble the minute I laid eyes on them," said Mr. Nuttybuddy. "Rustcoats–that's what they are–Rustcoats!"

"Rustcoats?" squeaked Zeek. "Do you think they could be Rustcoats?" asked Zeek—concern showing in his voice. He glanced at Bomber to see what his reaction was to Mr. Nuttybuddy's accusation. Of course, he couldn't tell a thing from Bomber's cold, steely stare at Mr. Nuttybuddy.

"Bomber?" squeaked Zeek, hoping for some reassurance.

"For all I know, they could be!" said Mr. Nuttybuddy.

"All you know is how to run off at the mouth," said Bomber.

Mr. Nuttybuddy opened his mouth to say something back to Bomber, but Bomber's look made Mr. Nuttybuddy hesitate for a few seconds.

Bomber continued, "So you think Christmas Bear is helping Rustcoats, do you? You think Silver Bear brought Rustcoats to the Summit?"

Mr. Nuttybuddy looked at Bomber but didn't say anything.

"Zeek, I don't think Mr. Nuttybuddy is going to be the one to help you gather the Circle to Cedar Rest. Mr. Nuttybuddy seems to be questioning Christmas Bear's judgment about the children. You go ahead and do the best you can without him. I will be taking him to Talon with his insinuations. Talon has more patience with his rantings than I do." Bomber had his face into Mr. Nuttybuddy's face again—only this time so close that Mr. Nuttybuddy backed into the Aspen and couldn't move because Bomber's sharp, imposing beak was against his nose.

"I...I....no...please...I...I didn't mean to imply...I don't think it's necessary...Bomber, you know I hate to fly...I'm sorry I..." Bomber interrupted Mr. Nuttybuddy again.

"Then keep your opinions to yourself and do as you are asked without complaining!" ordered Bomber as he backed away from Mr. Nuttybuddy. Mr. Nuttybuddy slumped down on his rump at the base of the tree.

"Mr. Nuttybuddy and I will get going right away, Bomber, ok?" offered Zeek. Bomber didn't respond—he was just staring at Mr. Nuttybuddy. "OK Bomber?" squeaked Zeek again.

"Yes," said Bomber, finally looking at Zeek. "You and Mr. Nuttybuddy need to get started right away. You have much to do and not much time to do it. Remember," he said looking at both of them, "you must have the Treetoppers at Cedar Rest before Christmas Bear finishes his rounds. The meeting will start as soon as Christmas Bear arrives."

Bomber flew off toward the Summit. Zeek and a shaken Mr. Nuttybuddy split up and began their assignment in Treetop.

———— ✳ ————

**A Scolding**

# Chapter 16:

# The Rounds

Christmas Bear stopped at a wide path at the beginning of a beautiful Blue Spruce forest and laid down. The scent of pine was so strong, it tickled Jonas' nose.

"I love that smell," muttered Jonas to himself.

"Smells like Christmas," said Rebekah.

"Smells like heaven," smiled Christmas Bear.

Just then, Stalker came up behind them carrying a dark green velvety sack draped over his back. He went over, dropped the sack at Christmas Bears feet, and then laid next to him.

"Rebekah and Jonas," called Christmas Bear as Stalker got settled, "climb up on Stalker's back." The Children hesitated at that command. Stalker didn't look like the type who wanted children climbing on him.

"Come on," said Christmas Bear gently, "We must be going."

Rebekah walked up beside Stalker. He was a big wolf, and even when he was lying down, he came up to Rebekah's waist. She motioned for Jonas to hop up on Stalker. Jonas came over and Rebekah gave him a boost up. She then climbed up next to Jonas. They could smell the pine scent on Stalker's hair.

Stalker surprised Rebekah and Jonas by immediately getting to his feet. They both had to grab handfuls of hair to keep from falling. Stalker leaned against Christmas Bear's side and the children leaned into Christmas Bear's fur. Christmas Bear's scent was stronger than Stalker's.

"Hop up," said Christmas Bear looking back at the children. "Just grab some fur and climb up—it doesn't hurt me."

Jonas grabbed deep handfuls of soft fur and worked his way onto Christmas Bear's back.

"Come up close to my neck, Jonas," said Christmas Bear. "You will find it easier to sit there. Rebekah, climb up and sit right behind him."

Rebekah did as she was told. As soon as she was in place, Christmas Bear told Stalker to run ahead and tell everyone he was starting down Sprucewalk. Stalker was off without a word. Christmas Bear picked up his sack and headed down the heavily forested path with Rebekah and Jonas gently rocking side to side in rhythm with Christmas Bear's gait.

Sprucewalk was a windy, downhill path through a forest of Blue Spruce Trees. After a few minutes on the path, Jonas leaned forward into Christmas Bear's fur to keep warm, and Rebekah leaned forward with her head on Jonas' back. They could hear the steady crunch of Christmas Bear's feet in the snow. They were so comfortable and were just starting to fall asleep when Christmas Bear spoke.

"Good evening, Hopper," said Christmas Bear cheerfully. "Nice to see you, Slipper."

Rebekah and Jonas sat up and looked to see who Hopper and Slipper were. Christmas Bear was slowing down and then stopped in front of two large rabbits on the path.

"Hello, Christmas Bear," both rabbits said in unison.

When they spotted Rebekah and Jonas, the smaller, light grey rabbit stepped a little behind the larger, dark grey one.

"You've got some strange looking things on your back there, Christmas Bear. Could they be miniature people?" asked the Dark grey rabbit.

"You could say that, Hopper," answered Christmas Bear. "They're children. The one in front is Jonas and behind him is Rebekah. I'm helping them find their way home. Rebekah and Jonas—this is Hopper and his wife Slipper."

Rebekah, Jonas, and the Rabbits nodded to each other in acknowledgement.

"I haven't seen people in Treetop since The Fall," said Hopper. "How did they get here? Why did they come?"

"I'm calling a meeting at Cedar Rest after my rounds to explain the whole thing," replied Christmas Bear. "I would like you to gather all the other male rabbits along Sprucewalk. I have a job for you that I will explain at the meeting. Can you do that for me?"

"I can and will," said Hopper.

"Can the ladies help out?" asked Slipper.

"You ladies will be helping us by tending your homes and families," smiled Christmas Bear. "The men can handle what needs to be done, and they shouldn't be gone too long doing it."

Christmas Bear started digging around in his sack and brought out a small bag of what looked like broken pieces of green cookies.

"Here is your present," said Christmas Bear, handing the bag to Hopper. "Merry Christmas!"

Christmas Bear started down Sprucewalk again. Rebekah and Jonas turned back to look at Hopper and Slipper.

"Thank you," they both said in unison. Hopper handed the bag to Slipper, said something, and Slipper disappeared into the trees. Hopper crossed the path and disappeared into the trees on the opposite side of the path.

After a few more minutes traveling down Sprucewalk, Christmas Bear stopped next to a large boulder. Almost immediately, two skunks came around from the back side of the boulder and greeted Christmas Bear.

"Merry Christmas," they said in unison as they walked up to Christmas Bear.

"Merry Christmas, Squirt. It's nice to see you, Duster," greeted Christmas Bear.

Duster looked up at Rebekah and Jonas and seemed to have a pleasant look on her face. Squirt hadn't noticed them until Duster nudged him and pointed. Squirt jumped slightly and began to turn and raise his tail.

"Whoa, Squirt. Don't even think about it!" exclaimed Christmas Bear. "They're friends, and they need our help."

Squirt stopped turning and lowered his tail.

"The last time I saw the likes of them we had trouble," said Squirt. "Why are they back?"

"I will explain all this at a meeting at Cedar Rest after my rounds. Squirt, I would like you to gather the male skunks for the meeting. Duster, you and the other lady skunks can tend to your homes and families. The men will only be needed for the morning. Oh," added Christmas Bear, "and here is your present."

Christmas Bear handed them a small bag of green cookie-like stuff similar to the one he gave the rabbits.

"Thank you," said Duster. She then looked at Squirt and said, "I'll see you tomorrow afternoon sometime." Duster then walked back into the forest and disappeared into the trees.

"You must hurry, Squirt," said Christmas Bear. "I have an important job for you all to do."

"I'll have everyone there," said Squirt. "When I tell everyone 'they' are back," nodding toward Rebekah and Jonas, "I won't be able to keep them away."

As Squirt walked off behind the boulder, Christmas Bear continued on down Sprucewalk.

Christmas Bear made several more stops with different animals and told them the same instructions and gave them the same present—that small bag of green cookie-like stuff. They met raccoons—Bandit and Ranger; owls—Hooter, Sniper, and Swoop; and beavers—Chipper and Dike. But the strangest meeting of all was yet to come.

Rebekah and Jonas started to doze off on Christmas Bear's back again when Christmas Bear let out a loud, strange growl. It was kind of a mixture of growling and singing. Rebekah and Jonas were jolted out of their drowsiness by the sound. There was absolute quiet, and then Christmas Bear let out another growl-sing. Then all was quiet again.

They waited a few minutes before they heard anything. Then they heard something like a distant wind, but not exactly. There was also a brushing sound and often a slight popping sound. Rebekah and Jonas could see nothing coming, but the combination of the wind, brushing, and popping sounds grew slightly louder. They waited. Christmas Bear just stood there looking at the trees in front of him.

Suddenly a black mass exploded from the trees from all directions. The air was filled with deep, scary buzzing. Large black hornets were everywhere. Their wings made the wind sound, when they passed through pine needles they made the brushing sound, and when they smacked into aspen leaves, they made the popping sound. The swarm of hornets was so thick the air was black. The noises were so loud that Rebekah and Jonas could hardly hear the other speak. They were terrified. They didn't like being around bees, and hornets were ten times worse. They clung to each other, closed their eyes, and tried to bury themselves in Christmas Bear's fur.

Then the overpowering noise stopped all at once, but not all was quiet. There was one deep buzz sound—and it was right over their heads. It was like when a mosquito is flying in your room at night and every once in a while it sounds like it's going to fly right into your ear. But this was no mosquito! The deep buzzing seemed to be a few feet over their heads one minute—then right by their ear the next. This went on for what seemed like forever to Rebekah and Jonas. Then there was complete silence.

"It's landed," Jonas whispered to Rebekah. "It must be close by."

"Jooonaaas," said Rebekah in a very frightened whisper, "I feel something crawling up my back!"

"Don't move," warned Jonas.

Rebekah could feel the crawling thing make its way toward her neck. Slowly.....closer....Rebekah was about ready to scream! The crawling thing stopped at the very top of Rebekah's collar. She could feel it moving around in the same spot—like going around in circles.

Then they heard the deep buzzing sound again above their heads. "He's off me," whispered Rebekah, but the buzzing stopped as quickly as it restarted.

"Rebekaaaaah," cried Jonas, "it's on me now!"

Jonas could feel the feet of the bug on his left arm. They were heavy feet, and they were making their way up his arm. *Don't move, Jonas!* he said to himself as the creature made its way to the top of his collar. It stopped just like it had on Rebekah. In a few minutes, it was off him and buzzing again—only this time a little farther away.

"I think you've terrified the Children, Zapper" said Christmas Bear. All Rebekah and Jonas heard in response to Christmas Bear was a bunch of buzzing.

"Yes, I understand," said Christmas Bear, "but you could have handled it differently. Scaring people is not supposed to be fun for you, and you are not supposed to be trying to get back at them for all the trouble they caused."

More buzzing.

Rebekah and Jonas began to slowly raise their faces from Christmas Bear's fur. They then began to peek around Christmas Bear's neck to see who Christmas Bear was talking to.

"They'll be glad to hear you won't do it again, Zapper!" Christmas Bear chuckled and the buzzing changed to sound like a higher tone buzz-chuckle.

When Rebekah and Jonas leaned over far enough, they saw the biggest, ugliest, blackest hornet they had ever seen in their lives. It was hovering about two feet from Christmas Bear's nose.

"That's Rebekah and Jonas peeking at you," said Christmas Bear, "they need our help to get home."

"Rebekah and Jonas," Christmas Bear said—still looking at the hornet, "this is Zapper, the captain of the hornets. You don't need to be frightened of him or his swarm. He is here to help us deal with the animals from Rustcoat."

Louder, deeper buzzing came from Zapper.

"Yes, you heard right. I've called a meeting at Cedar Rest after my rounds. I would like you and your hornets to attend."

More buzzing.

"No, I don't think we need to bother the bees or wasps at this time. Your hornets can handle what needs to be done. I'll see you shortly at Cedar Rest."

Zapper rose vertically 30 feet in an instant. He hovered for a few seconds and then the air was filled with the sound of thousands of hornets as they came from the trees and filled the air. Zapper and his army of hornets flew off in a black cloud. Rebekah and Jonas could hear the brushing and popping sounds fade in the distance. Soon the forest was quiet again.

"You two should try to get some sleep now. "You've had an unusually exciting night, and it will take some time to get to Cedar Rest from here."

Christmas Bear started walking down the path again. Rebekah and Jonas rocked gently side to side in time with his gait. They were thinking about all the animals they had met along the path and were wondering about what was going to happen at the meeting at Cedar Rest. All the thinking and rocking made them drowsy again. They bent forward—Jonas leaning on Christmas Bear's neck and Rebekah leaning against Jonas' back. The comforting scent of pine filled their nostrils as they fell off to sleep.

**Sprucewalk**

# Chapter 17:

# Cedar Rest

A loud howling woke Rebekah and Jonas from a very sound sleep. They sat up and saw a wolf ahead of them with his nose pointed to the sky. Animals were scampering from everywhere heading to a clearing past the howling wolf. This was the end of Sprucewalk. They had arrived at Cedar Rest.

Cedar Rest was a spacious clearing surrounded by Cedar and Spruce trees on three sides. The west side of Cedar Rest overlooked a slope descending all the way down the mountainside. The slope was initially very steep but gradually flattened out about half way down. Trees grew thick on the steep part of the slope, but then the trees thinned out. The lower mountainside was covered with brush like Rebekah and Jonas had at home. Cedar Rest was full of large flat rocks of slightly differing heights that fit together like a big puzzle. Running the length of almost the entire north end was a huge boulder about seven feet tall. Rebekah and Jonas thought it resembled a whale. They had never seen a boulder like it.

Christmas Bear stopped at the howling wolf. Animals were streaming past them taking up places on all the lower flat rocks—bears, wolves, eagles, owls, bobcats, beavers, porcupines, chipmunks, squirrels, rabbits, raccoons, skunks, wolverines, rattlesnakes, and a cougar. Most of them stared long and hard at Rebekah and Jonas as they passed them.

They were clearly not friendly stares. Rebekah and Jonas were glad they were on Christmas Bear's back.

"Good morning, Pacer," said Christmas Bear kindly. "Thank you for announcing our arrival. Is everyone here?"

"All but the hornets."

Pacer looked at Rebekah and Jonas with pale grey eyes.

"This is Rebekah and Jonas, Pacer. You will be guiding them back to Treetop Circle shortly."

Pacer nodded as he stared at Rebekah and Jonas. "All should go well." was all Pacer said.

Rebekah and Jonas didn't know they would be going back to Treetop Circle so soon, and Pacer was a wolf they had never seen before. They discussed how Pacer must be an important wolf if Christmas Bear trusted him to bring them back to Treetop Circle. Still, it was another unexpected journey with a stranger that made them both a little anxious. Could going back to the Circle be the first leg of their journey back home? They both hoped so. Rebekah and Jonas wanted to know more about Pacer and their return trip with him. However, before they could ask anything, Christmas Bear walked past Pacer and entered Cedar Rest.

As they entered the rocky clearing, Rebekah and Jonas got their first glimpse of the huge boulder on the north side. Just below the right side of the stone sat Silver Bear. When he spotted Christmas Bear with the children he rose to his feet and smiled at them. On top of the stone on the left and right sides stood Talon and Stalker; they weren't smiling at anyone.

Christmas Bear walked over to Silver Bear, and they exchanged greetings. Christmas Bear then laid down. Pacer had followed him over to the stone and laid down against Christmas Bear.

"Climb down, Children," said Christmas Bear. "Stay near Silver Bear while I address the warriors."

"But…well…could we just stay on your back?" asked Rebekah. "We don't see too many friendly faces here and…"

"You are safe here. You must remember these animals haven't seen a human in a long time, and the last time they did see one, bad things happened here. Stay near Silver Bear," repeated Christmas Bear.

Rebekah and Jonas did as they were told. They slid off Christmas Bear's back and on to Pacer's back. They then slid off Pacer's back to the ground. Silver Bear was seated on his hind legs with his front paws extended out like he was offering a hug—which he was. Rebekah and Jonas ran up to Silver Bear and hugged him tightly. Silver Bear's front legs embraced Rebekah and Jonas affectionately. Even though most of the other animals were still giving them cold stares, they felt very safe next to Silver Bear.

They stood with Silver Bear as Christmas Bear climbed to the top of the huge boulder and positioned himself between Stalker and Talon. He sat and looked out over the animals. He waited while all the animal conversations came to a halt. Although more quiet now, most of the animals were fidgety and looking all around as if they were expecting something. Talon and Stalker remained motionless as they stared at the animals in front of them.

Rebekah and Jonas then heard a familiar sound. It was a sound something like a distant breeze, but not exactly. There was also a brushing sound and often a slight popping sound. They knew the hornets were coming. So did everyone else. The animals on the flat rocks seemed a bit uneasy.

Suddenly, just like on Sprucewalk, the overpowering sound of thousands of hornets filled Cedar Rest. Many of the animals ducked low on the rocks as the hornets burst through the trees and swarmed about them. It took a few minutes for the hornets to find their places in the surrounding trees, and they all seemed to find it at once. In an instant there was quiet.

"We're all here now so we will begin," announced Christmas Bear in a powerful voice. "Sunrise will be here in a few hours and we must all be in position by then. We've got trouble coming to Treetop." Christmas Bear paused to make sure he had everyone's attention. Then he said, "Rustcoats will attempt to violate Treetop's boundaries today."

There was a great murmuring in the crowd of animals.

Christmas Bear interrupted the murmurs, "I know this concerns you, as it should, but I can also tell you that it is a good sign for us—not a bad one."

The murmuring started again, but louder this time.

"Excuse me, Christmas Bear, but may I ask why you believe this is a good sign for us?" asked a raccoon on the flat rock farthest back from Christmas Bear.

"That's a good question, and I will take some time now to explain that to you all," answered Christmas Bear. "As you all know, a third of the original Treetop animals were banished to Rustcoat after The Fall."

Even after thousands of years since The Fall, you could feel the heaviness of that memory weighing on the Treetoppers. Everyone was so still, you could have heard a pine needle snap.

Christmas Bear continued, "The return of the humans to Treetop is a sign from God that things are about to take a turn for good in Rustcoat. You see, not all humans living in Rustcoat are Rustcoats. Some of them belong to the Lord, and more and more of them are finally beginning to act like it. In order to assist God's people in taking dominion of the earth, we have been tasked with eliminating the original Treetop rebels from Rustcoat. The Lord has graciously arranged for many of those rebels to come to us this morning to begin the purge."

A paw shot up on a front rock to ask a question. A wolverine was recognized by Christmas Bear, "Yes, Tussle."

"What are the rebels trying to accomplish by coming here?"

"Yesterday morning they tried to keep these children out of Treetop so God's message to begin the purge wouldn't reach us. I now suspect they will try to delay their return home. By keeping us occupied with the children's safety, they hope to keep us from starting our mission against them. Therefore, it is very important that we get Rebekah and Jonas safely home today." Christmas Bear paused as paws started popping up all over Cedar Rest with more questions.

"Instead of answering each of your questions individually, I am going to have Stalker outline our plan so you all know what we're about to do. Most of your questions will be answered once our plan is explained to you. Stalker?"

The crowd of animals began to murmur again as Christmas Bear and Stalker changed places. The murmuring stopped immediately as Stalker let out a low growl as he sat down to address them.

"We only have a short time to get ready for the Rustcoats," said Stalker. "They will be at the borders of Treetop in a few hours. The Rustcoats are being led by wolves you know—Skull and Dameon."

This news brought gasps and whispers throughout Cedar Rest. Stalker let out his low growl again and everyone became still.

"Skull and Dameon are coming with several hundred animals–a sorry assortment of mostly wolves and coyotes. They'll be coming from the west right here at the foot of Cedar Rest. Talon's squad has done some reconnaissance, and they report that Skull is not attempting to hide his advance toward Treetop. We believe that means they think we aren't expecting their advance so soon. They think they have the advantage of surprise on their side. We will take advantage of their mistaken belief."

Stalker stood on all fours and began to slowly walk back and forth on the big rock as he revealed the plan.

"Mr. Nuttybuddy, Zeek, Jitter?" called out Stalker.

"We're here, sir!" said Zeek chattering and flipping his tail to get Stalkers attention.

"Zeek, you, Jitter, and Mr. Nuttybuddy are to take your chipmunks and squirrels and hide yourselves in the trees all along the perimeter of Treetop. If your soldiers see any Rustcoats coming from anywhere other than the west, send one representative from that danger area and have them report to Silver Bear's home. Everyone else is to remain at their posts in the trees to see if we are being invaded from other locations. Squirrels and chipmunks will remain silent in the trees if any Rustcoats pass under them. Under no circumstances are you to engage the enemy or let them know of your presence."

"Hopper?" called Stalker.

Hopper thumped his hind foot on the rock he was sitting on with some other rabbits and said, "Present, sir!"

"Hopper, you and your rabbits have one of the most dangerous jobs. You will be the first to engage the enemy up close. You will lure the Rustcoats into the trap we will set for them. Your soldiers will be the bait for our trap."

The rabbits on the rock looked at each other briefly at that news, but said nothing and waited for Stalker to continue.

"When we finish our meeting here, Hopper, you will take your forces and hide yourselves in the brush along the border of Treetop directly in the path of the invasion. Mask your scent before you get to your assigned area. I want the Rustcoats to be completely surprised by your presence. When they are right on top of you, I want you to scatter and run toward Treetop. I want you to stay visible to the Rustcoats. I want them to chase you."

Rebekah and Jonas looked at each other with baffled looks on their faces.

"What does 'mask' their scent mean?" Jonas whispered to Rebekah.

Before Rebekah could say she didn't know what it meant, Silver Bear leaned over and explained.

"Treetoppers can control their scent. If we want to be undetectable by other animals, we hide our scent completely. Rebel animals know what the pine scent means, so we can choose whether or not we want them to know where or who we are."

"Wow," whispered Rebekah and Jonas in unison.

Rebekah and Jonas turned their attention back to the meeting as Hopper raised his paw. When he was recognized by Stalker, he asked, "Sir, how close is 'on top of us' before you want us to run?"

Stalker always looked serious, but he even looked more serious now.

"Hopper, you are the key to our plan. Skull's troops are tough, but they are not well disciplined. I'm sure they were told to stay together and advance cautiously once they reached Treetop's border. I need you and your soldiers to get them to break ranks. Striker and his army of snakes will be hidden in the brush east of where you will instigate the chase. You must get the Rustcoats to fan out and chase you, and you must stay ahead of your pursuers until you pass the snakes."

Hopper raised his paw again. Stalker nodded for him to ask another question.

"How will we know when we've passed the snakes?"

"You will hear squeals of pain and fear as we attack the Rustcoats while their focus is on you," replied Striker as he raised his head above the rock Hopper was sitting on.

Hopper jumped back and knocked into some rabbits next to him as Striker suddenly appeared by Hopper's rock. Striker had been coiled in front of the rock before the meeting started, but he was so still and blended with his surroundings so well that no one had noticed him.

"Striker, you scared the wits out of me!" said an embarrassed Hopper.

"Didn't mean to," said Striker, "but that is exactly what we will do to the Rustcoats. You will make our surprise attack even more effective with your diversion."

The exchange between Hopper and Striker had disrupted the order of the meeting and Stalker started to growl again. Everyone became silent and gave him their attention.

Stalker addressed Striker, "You must let the Rustcoats overrun your frontline snakes, Striker. I know that is dangerous, but we can't risk scaring them off until they are completely in our trap. When they reach your rear line warriors, I will howl. That will be the signal for your strikes to begin. You should be able to take out a good portion of their forces throughout the battlefield if we can work this right."

"We'll be able to wait," assured Striker.

Stalker nodded to Striker and continued, "Squirt and Dagger, I need your skunks and porcupines to form skirmish lines on the north and south edges of the battlefield. I suggest you alternate skunk-porcupine-skunk-porcupine for a good mix of our defenses. I want to keep the Rustcoats in a narrow fighting area. If they begin to flee to the outer edges of the field, let them have it."

Dagger looked over to Squirt and said, "Better keep a few feet distance between our ranks so your folks don't get quilled. Those harpoons of ours come off easily when we're riled. Wouldn't want to get sprayed for a mishap."

Squirt smiled and said, "Good idea. We'll space ourselves as you suggest. We'll all benefit from the longer skirmish lines that will result."

Squirt raised and lowered his tail as if saluting Stalker to acknowledge that he and Dagger will form the skirmish lines as he ordered.

Stalker continued, "The snake attack should halt the advance of the Rustcoats, and the confusion will draw the attention of Skull and his lieutenants. Striker, tell your snakes to give no warning—they are to strike and move closer to Treetop after each strike. When chaos has spread throughout their ranks, sound your rattle to tell your troops to get out of there—head back to Cedar Rest. Before the Rustcoats are able to regroup and continue their advance, the hornets will strafe them."

At the mention of the hornets, the trees around Cedar Rest buzzed as the hornets acknowledged their instructions.

"Zapper, I want you to harass the Rustcoat troops until they retreat past where the first line of snakes attacked them. Once you have driven them back that far, you and your swarms should return to Cedar Rest."

Zapper flew down from his tree, hovered in front of Stalker for a few seconds buzzing loudly, and then flew back to his place.

"Grizzle and Pouncer, have your wolverines and bobcats take up positions behind the skirmish lines of the skunks and porcupines. If the integrity of their lines are threatened, you will eliminate that threat.

Stalker continued, "Talon and his eagles, along with the owls and hawks, will then swoop down on the Rustcoats to keep them near our border. We don't want them leaving and we don't want them advancing on Treetop.

"Finally, as they are kept in place and distracted by the flyers, the bears and wolves will advance with me slowly from our tree line. We will try to get as close as we can without being noticed. While they are being distracted, we will attack swiftly and finish things.

"Whiskers, I need you and Shadow to maintain a constant patrol of Treetop's interior. You two will handle any problems there as they arise." Stalker paused. "Where is Shadow by the way? I haven't seen him this morning."

"I believe he has been given an assignment that he is tending to. Don't worry about the interior. Shadow and I will take care of it." Stalker nodded to Whiskers and moved on.

"Those of you who are not given a specific assignment in this battle will remain at Cedar Rest in case you are needed for later deployment. Are there any questions from anyone?"

Grizzle, the wolverine, stood up and asked in a gruff voice, "Are there any plans for prisoners?"

"There will be no prisoners and none will be allowed to escape," said Stalker flatly. "This is especially important for Skull, their leader. Our task of eliminating the rebellious animals in Rustcoat will go much easier if we can eliminate him in this first battle."

"Any more questions?"

"Why must we eliminate the rebels in Rustcoat?" asked Sniper, a large owl perched in a tree to Stalker's left. "What have they done to necessitate their removal at this stage of the dominion struggle?"

"Surprisingly, the rebels, through deception and manipulation, have been able to convince a considerable number of humans that animal life is just as precious—even more precious—than human life," answered Stalker. "Since many men no longer believe they are created in the image of God, they open themselves up to believing just about anything. The rebels took advantage of this foolishness and used what they call 'domestic' animals to distract people from their dominion tasks. Many people would now rather develop a relationship with a puppy than with their neighbor, their children, or even their spouse. The time has come for the rebel animals to be punished for their sinful deceptions."

"Anyone else with a question?

Cedar Rest was quiet. The mission and their parts in it were clear, and all were anxious to put the plan into action.

"Very well. Striker, you are dismissed to join your snakes. Hopper, you and your rabbits are dismissed to take up your positions in the brush. Squirt and Dagger, you are clear to form your lines. Grizzle and Pouncer, you are free to take up your support positions."

Everyone began to move all at once. In a matter of a few minutes, Cedar Rest was almost deserted except for Christmas Bear, Silver Bear, Stalker, Talon, Rebekah, and Jonas.

"Gather around me," said Christmas Bear as he motioned with his paw to those remaining.

Talon and Stalker were already on the rock. Silver Bear, Rebekah and Jonas climbed up and formed a circle with the others.

"Pacer will be back shortly with the rest of the wolves and bears," said Christmas Bear. "As soon as he returns, he will take Rebekah and Jonas back to the Treetop Circle Path."

Rebekah and Jonas had been caught up listening to the battle plans and had not given a thought to getting back home during the briefing. Hearing about going home made them feel happy, but at the same time, they felt like they were leaving a battle they should help fight.

"We can stay and help out if you want," offered Rebekah.

"It doesn't seem right that we should leave you without helping in some way," added Jonas.

Christmas Bear smiled at them. "You must remember what the battle is all about. Our primary mission cannot begin until you are safely home, remember?"

Rebekah and Jonas nodded as they remembered what Christmas Bear had told them.

"After Pacer gets you to Treetop Circle, he will give you directions on how to get to the path that leads to your home. You must follow his directions carefully."

"Pacer's not going to go with us all the way home?" asked Rebekah with concern in her voice.

Christmas Bear motioned for Rebekah and Jonas to come to him. As they got close, Christmas Bear engulfed them with the biggest bear hug they had ever had. The pine smell of his fur made them feel safe and content. He looked down at them and said, "You must always remember to trust God completely. Pacer might make you feel safe, but he couldn't save you—even if he was with you the whole way home—unless God willed it. Know that God is with you always everywhere.

There is no protector better than Him. No foe can beat Him. You will never be in any danger where He isn't with you to give you His peace."

"I know what you say is true," said Rebekah, "but it's hard to remember it and make it real when you need it the most."

"Yeah," agreed Jonas, "when things are good and safe, we talk about it and are thankful for God's promise to care for us always. But as soon as things don't go the way we want them to go, we complain, we get angry, we get fearful, and oftentimes we make things worse for ourselves."

"The fact that you know this truth, and that you struggle with your failure to apply it is the sign of the true believer. You are young and yet you possess true knowledge and faith that most adults can't grasp. Rejoice in this precious gift that God has given you—in all circumstances rejoice."

Christmas Bear turned his attention to the others in the group. "Talon, your flyers have done well; Stalker, excellent briefing! Silver Bear, you can go on ahead and I'll catch up."

As Christmas Bear was talking, Pacer entered Cedar Rest with a large group of Treetoppers following him. Pacer stopped at the foot of the rock and awaited instructions. There was not enough room at Cedar Rest to hold all the warriors. The forest all around the meeting place was overflowing with wolves, bears, wolverines, and bobcats as far and Rebekah and Jonas could see.

Christmas Bear addressed the new group. "Thank you for coming so quickly. I know Pacer has briefed you on what we are about to do. We are about an hour away from battle. Rest in the area until you are called to form up."

What amazed Rebekah and Jonas the most about this large group of warriors was the fact that they hadn't made a sound approaching the area. Rebekah and Jonas hadn't noticed Pacer or the others with him until they actually entered Cedar Rest. It was incredible that so many animals could be so quiet when moving together. They also marveled at the orderliness of the numerous and varied warriors.

"Pacer, you can take Rebekah and Jonas to Treetop Circle now. They must be well on their way home by the time this battle starts."

Christmas Bear hugged the children again with a long bear hug. Rebekah and Jonas started to tear up as the thought entered their minds that they might not see Christmas Bear again. Christmas Bear released them from his grip, smiled at them and said, "Remember to trust God always." He then gestured for them to get off the rock and be on their way.

Rebekah and Jonas turned and climbed off the rock. They ended up right in front of Pacer.

"We must get going. Treetop Circle is this way," said Pacer as he turned and headed east out of Cedar Rest.

Rebekah and Jonas looked around for Silver Bear so they could say good bye to him. He was nowhere in sight. Talon and Stalker were gone, too.

"Come on," said Pacer kindly, "everybody is about their business and we must be, too."

Pacer led the way out of Cedar Rest and into the forest. Rebekah and Jonas stopped and took their last glimpses of the meeting place and Christmas Bear on the big rock. They then continued through the wolves and bears that were lying all over the ground. There were wolves and bears as far as they could see in the forest. All the warriors looked at them as they passed. There wasn't a mean look on any faces now. They all seemed fierce, but kind and gentle all at the same time. It took a good 20 minutes to pass through the warriors and get to clear forest. Rebekah and Jonas followed behind Pacer as he meandered through the trees. Their minds wandered back and forth between thoughts of home and thoughts of the battle soon to be fought. They prayed for victory and safe travel.

**Call To Meeting**

# Chapter 18:

# Much Will Be Demanded

Christmas Bear, Talon, and Stalker stood in silence at the edge of Cedar Rest looking down upon the battlefield. As they watched and waited, an eagle dropped out of the shadows and landed next to Talon.

"They are about thirty minutes from the border," said Bomber as he touched down. "There are about 400 of them. Looks like mostly wolves and coyotes. There are a few bears and bobcats, but not many. It was too dark to be more exact, but that's how it appears."

"Did you identify any of the leaders?" asked Talon.

"No. We don't know who the leaders are yet. We probably won't have enough light to identify them until they get here. We'd have to get too close to identify them now, and I didn't want to take a chance on spoiling our ambush."

"Good. That was the right decision."

"I'll go and alert the warriors that we will be going down the hill soon," said Stalker.

"And I'm going back to monitor them and will let you know as soon as I can identify the Rustcoat leaders," said Bomber.

Stalker went in one direction and Bomber flew off in another. Christmas Bear and Talon stood alone in the predawn darkness.

"The children will do fine," said Talon–knowing Christmas Bear was thinking of Rebekah and Jonas. "They are strong for young ones."

"Yes," said Christmas Bear, "they are delightful children. They were picked for this assignment because they are strong. The strong ones get the toughest jobs. We must trust Him just as they must trust Him. Thank God all of this is in His hands."

"Amen," said Talon.

Pacer had gotten a little ahead of Rebekah and Jonas. He was waiting for the children at the top of a gentle hill. Rebekah and Jonas were tired, and the hill seemed like a mountain to them. Even though they had gotten a little nap while riding on Christmas Bear, this had been an especially tiring night and day.

"I want to rest," said Jonas. "I wonder how much farther we have to go."

"We can't get too far behind Pacer," said Rebekah, "and we have to think of the others. The sooner we're home, the better for them."

The children staggered up the snowy hill toward Pacer, looking down at their feet so they didn't have to look at the hill as they climbed it.

"One step at a time," panted Rebekah, "one step at a time."

Jonas was blowing out big frosty growly breaths each time he stomped down the snow. He was pretending he was a Raptor looking for something to eat. He figured if he couldn't rest, he was going to keep his mind off the climb.

Finally they reached Pacer, who they found sitting on a wide path. It was the path around Treetop Circle.

"You have done well," said Pacer. "We have covered a lot of ground in a short time. That was the last hill you will have to climb. The rest of your journey will be level or downhill."

"Do we have time to rest a bit? Just a really short one?" pleaded Rebekah

Jonas plopped down at Rebekah's feet looking hopefully at Pacer.

"I'm afraid that would not be a good idea," answered Pacer. The Rustcoats must have reached our border by now. You must not delay."

Rebekah and Jonas had expected that answer. Rebekah sat next to Jonas as Pacer continued talking.

"This is as far as I can go with you. I must tend to other pressing matters. You are to follow the Treetop path in that direction," as he nodded toward the southeast. "When you come to a fork in the road, take the lower path; that will be the same path you climbed with Silver Bear to get here. It's very important that you stay on that path. Any questions?" asked Pacer.

"How far to the fork," sighed Jonas, resigning himself to going it alone with Rebekah from there.

"Not far," said Pacer as he started back down the hill they had just climbed. "Stay on the path!" shouted Pacer as he disappeared down the hill among the trees.

Rebekah and Jonas stood there staring down the pine hill for a few moments. "Well," said Rebekah, "let's get going. After all, this is Treetop. Just how dangerous could it be?"

"They wouldn't leave us alone if there was any danger," said Jonas assuredly.

"You wouldn't think so," replied Rebekah.

Treetop was completely still. The only sound that could be heard was Rebekah's and Jonas' feet crunching snow as they started on what they hoped to be the last leg of their journey home.

**Returning to Treetop Circle**

# Chapter 19:

# Situational Awareness

In the darkness just before morning, Stalker led the Treetop warriors over the edge of Cedar Rest and down the steep spruce covered hillside. Bears, wolves, bobcats, and wolverines poured over the side of the hill like a waterfall. Christmas Bear watched as his army took up their positions just inside the tree line in the middle of the hill.

Past the tree line, the hill leveled out to a wide high brush covered field. You couldn't see it, but that lower field was full of rabbits, skunks, porcupines, and rattlesnakes. There was no talking—not even a whisper. They knew their assignments, and they were patiently waiting for their enemies to walk into the trap they had set for them.

In Cedar Rest, Christmas Bear was praying for the safety of his soldiers on the field of battle, and for the safety of the children on their journey home. *…and please, Father, give them safe passage home. Please give them this in Jesus' precious name."*

When he finished his prayer, he turned away from the battlefield and walked off into the forest.

Mr. Nuttybuddy was mumbling to himself as he raced through the pines and firs toward the southeast border of Treetop. Squirrels and chipmunks had passed news down the perimeter line that there was a breach of security there. *Why does there always have to be trouble? Why can't things just go right for a change?* thought Mr. Nuttybuddy .

Zeek was running northwest with news of the breach. He had already talked with the chipmunk where the breach occurred and was trying to intercept Mr. Nuttybuddy to pass on the information. Zeek was paying attention to his surroundings and saw Mr. Nuttybuddy coming straight toward him from some distance away. However, Mr. Nuttybuddy was too busy complaining to himself to know what was going on around him, so he didn't see Zeek.

Zeek couldn't call out to Mr. Nuttybuddy because he was concerned about giving away their positions. He wasn't sure where the Rustcoats were, and he wasn't taking any chances. Zeek figured Mr. Nuttybuddy would see him as he got closer. Zeek was sitting on a branch in the open as Mr. Nuttybuddy approached. To Zeek's surprise, Mr. Nuttybuddy raced right past him.

Zeek immediately began to chase Mr. Nuttybuddy, quickly caught up to him, and lightly tapped him on his back. Mr. Nuttybuddy let out a muffled screech, jumped sideways off the branch he was running on and fell to the ground. He landed on his back with a dull thud.

Zeek looked down at Mr. Nuttybuddy and had to hold his hand over his mouth to keep from laughing out loud. Mr. Nuttybuddy was dazed for a moment, then focused on Zeek, scowled and shook his fist at him. Mr. Nuttybuddy quickly got to his feet and scampered up to Zeek in the tree he just fell from.

"Are you trying to kill me?!" asked Mr. Nuttybuddy in a low, hoarse whisper.

"No, I'm trying to save you some time. I have just come from the breach with some additional news."

"You didn't have to scare me like that!" scolded Mr. Nuttybuddy in the same hoarse whisper.

"I **did** so," protested Zeek. "You ran right by me. You were lost to this world. You seemed to be mumbling to yourself—you were complaining about something, weren't you?"

Mr. Nuttybuddy was embarrassed that Zeek caught him being careless. "Never mind what I was doing," said Mr. Nuttybuddy, trying to regain his composure. Give me the news!" he demanded.

"Three wolves crossed the southeast Treetop border about twenty minutes ago. The sentry didn't get a good look at them. It was dark, and they had already crossed the border before they were noticed. The sentries in the area heard noises behind them in Treetop. When one of them went to investigate, he was only able to see their shadowy figures disappear up an embankment. The sentry didn't want to leave his part of the border unguarded too long, so he went back and had the information passed down the line to me."

"You all did the right thing," said Mr. Nuttybuddy. "I'll get this information to Christmas Bear right away. You try to find those border crossers and see if you can find out where they are headed and what they are up to."

"Will do," said Zeek.

Mr. Nuttybuddy headed swiftly back toward Treetop Circle. Zeek headed back to see if he could find the trespassers.

Rebekah and Jonas walked silently side by side down Treetop Circle Path. It was cold and quiet. Even though it was too dark to see color well, the eerie, dark grey hue of the very early morning was beautiful and peaceful.

The peace was broken by the loud snap of a twig. Rebekah and Jonas froze instantly to listen.

"What was that?" asked Jonas.

"It sounded like a twig breaking," said Rebekah.

They both turned toward the direction of the noise and stood absolutely still to see if they could hear or see something. They stood there a few minutes, but heard nothing further.

"Maybe it was a falling pine cone," suggested Jonas.

"Could have been," agreed Rebekah, "but falling pine cones usually land with a thud when they hit the ground. They often bounce and roll a little, too. What we heard sounded like dry wood snapping. I think we would have heard a different kind of noise from a falling cone."

They stood there for a few minutes more, but they heard no other sounds.

"Hello? ....... Is anybody there?" asked Rebekah. There was no response.

"It has to be somebody in Treetop," said Jonas. "It shouldn't be anybody to worry about."

"Hello? Is anybody there?" said Rebekah, a little louder this time. Still there was no response. "A Treetopper would answer us," reasoned Rebekah.

"Maybe nobody's there," said Jonas hopefully. "Besides, we just left Pacer a little while ago. How could somebody bad get this far in Treetop so quickly?"

"You're probably right. It was probably nobody, but it was an awfully loud snap."

They stood there for a few more minutes listening.

"If you are a Treetopper, come on out. Silver Bear and Christmas Bear know we are here. We're friends" said Jonas.

Still no response.

"Let's go," said Rebekah.

Rebekah and Jonas continued on down the path, but Rebekah kept looking back to see if she could get a glimpse of something.

"If you think 'it was nobody,'" said Jonas, "why do you keep looking back like you expect to see somebody."

"I said it was '**probably** nobody," retorted Rebekah. "It was **probably** nothing."

"I was **just** asking," mocked Jonas with a hint of a smile.

As they walked down the path, a pair of dark green eyes tracked their movements. When Rebekah and Jonas were just about out of sight, the big cougar cautiously followed after them. He would have to be more careful with his footing if he didn't want them to know he was trailing them. *They're wary for a couple of little kids,* he thought to himself as he made his way between the trees about thirty yards off the path.

It was still dark when the first line of Rustcoats stopped at the border of Treetop. They had been instructed to stop at the border to wait for the rest of their army to catch up.

"Hold up!" yelled a mangy wolf as he trotted along the border of Treetop. "Hold up!" he shouted again.

The wolves and coyotes began to sit or lie down where they were. Most were moaning or grumbling about being hungry or thirsty from their long walk. There appeared to be no concern about making noise. They were not on their guard.

"Fan out! Fan out!" barked another lead wolf. The second line of Rustcoats had reached the border and were being told to take up positions on either side of the first group.

Hopper was in a bush not more than twenty yards from those foul creatures. He watched as they spread out down the border about one hundred yards north and south of his position. He sat quietly and watched as the third and fourth line of Rustcoats arrived. He was trying to come up with a good way of surprising the greatest number of Rustcoats all at the same time. He didn't just want a few enemies chasing his rabbits, he wanted the whole army distracted. After thinking for several minutes, he turned to the four rabbits immediately behind him.

"Skippy and Jumper," whispered Hopper, "I have to ask you to do something very risky. I've got to get somebody behind the enemy. If we're going to surprise them all at once, we need to run through their ranks from back to front and from side to side. It will have to be done with lighting speed, and it will have to be done all together at my signal."

"What signal?" asked Skippy.

I will give the rabbit death scream. When I do, I will show myself to the front line of Rustcoats. This should confuse them for a moment. When you hear the scream, you must launch your troopers through the enemy—Skippy from the north side and Jumper from the south."

How much time do we have to get around the Rustcoats?" asked Jumper.

"You have until sunrise," answered Hopper. "I won't give the scream until the sun is completely above the eastern mountain—unless the Rustcoats begin advancing on Treetop before then. If you hear the scream before sunrise, you'll have to begin your charge through them from wherever you are. We have to cause mass confusion and get them to chase us through the snakes,"

"Zaggit," continued Hopper, "I need you and Twitch to go down our lines and tell the rest of the rabbits to show themselves to the Rustcoats at my scream. We must keep the attention of their front troops on us. We're to hold our positions until we see Skippy's and Jumper's groups bust through the front line of Rustcoats. Then we all break away back toward the snakes. Most of the Rustcoats should be on our tails. They are undisciplined and hungry. They will be thinking of an easy meal and not battle formation or an ambush. Any questions?"

"We're on it," said Skippy as he, Jumper, Zaggit, and Twitch disappeared into the brush.

Hopper turned his attention to the Rustcoats. He prayed that they would stay put until Skippy and Jumper could get around them.

**Passing Intel**

# Chapter 20:

# Improvise

Stalker looked down on the Rustcoats from the tree line as they gathered on the border. It was dark, but his night vision was unequalled and he saw their every move. He saw some rabbits sneaking across the border of Treetop and flanking the enemy on both the north and south sides of the battlefield.

"What is Hopper up to?" Stalker muttered to himself.

Pouncer was watching them too. "It looks like they are going to try to get around them and surprise them on multiple sides."

"That's very risky."

"Yes, but pretty smart, too," replied Pouncer. "There are a lot of Rustcoats down there, and they are spread out. If the rabbits can start the chase from the enemy's rear and middle ranks, it could cause more confusion and participation than simply getting the front line to chase them hoping the rest would follow. It's a brilliant move."

Zeek had quickly, but quietly maneuvered through the trees and had settled in a low, wide pine tree near the top of a ravine. Knowing he didn't have time to check all of southeast Treetop for the intruders, he decided to watch the hillside he would use if he were trying to sneak in. The hillside was heavily forested and had several ravines running up its face. The ravines were perfect for climbing the hill unnoticed. He had only been sitting for a short time when he heard something coming his way.

*I knew it,* he said to himself as he hunkered close to the trunk and watched.

In a moment, three figures emerged from bushes about thirty yards from the tree. It was still too dark to see well, but Zeek could tell there were three wolves. The three stood silently for a while looking around and sniffing the air. Then the biggest wolf continued up the hill with the other two following. When they were about twenty feet from Zeek's tree, he almost let out a gasp. He recognized the lead wolf. It was Skull. His two companions were Stickers and Weed.

Skull was a lead rebel of The Fall. When all the rebel animals were forced from Treetop, most left in sorrow and shame—but not Skull. Zeek could still picture him snarling at the lines of loyal animals as he was forced to the top of the original Summit. Head high, tail high, his excessive pride and arrogance were on display for all to see. Skull gave him the shivers.

"How much farther do you think we have to go before we reach the path?" complained Stickers.

"It's about a mile or so to the west," answered Skull gruffly. "We'll start heading west at the top of this hill."

"Do you think Creeper will find them?" asked Weed.

"I wouldn't have sent him ahead if I didn't!" snapped Skull.

Skull stopped at the base of the tree that Zeek was in. He looked around again and sniffed the air. Stickers and Weed began to sit down.

"On your feet!" ordered Skull. "We have no time for rest. We have got to get to the path as soon as we can. Keep your ears open for Creeper's scream. He said he'd scream when he had them where we're supposed to meet up."

Skull turned west and quietly disappeared into the bushes with his two companions.

Zeek immediately headed toward Silver Bear's house. After

overhearing Weed and Skull talking about Creeper, he now knew there were four Rustcoats in Treetop, not three! *Creeper snuck in unnoticed* he thought to himself. He didn't know exactly what path or meeting place Skull was talking about, but he figured Silver Bear would know. He also had to get the word out that a rebel cougar was somewhere in Treetop hunting the children.

Mr. Nuttybuddy arrived at Silver Bear's house and gave a loud chatter at the door. In a few seconds, Mrs. Silver Bear opened the door and let him in. Silver Bear and Christmas Bear were sitting by the fireplace in the sitting room across from the kitchen. Mr. Nuttybuddy and Mrs. Silver Bear joined them.

"There's been a breach of the southeast border of Treetop," said an out of breath Mr. Nuttybuddy. "Zeek reported that the sentry saw three wolves heading toward the Circle."

"That's good news," said Christmas Bear. "Thank you for bringing it to us promptly, Mr. Nuttybuddy."

"Good news?" said Mr. Nuttybuddy. "Good news!?" We're being invaded from the west and the southeast and this is good news? Is it something you bears eat that makes you think this way?" asked the exasperated squirrel.

"Mr. Nuttybuddy!" said Mrs. Silver Bear—getting nose to nose with the squirrel. "While you are in my house, you will speak respectfully of bears, and you will be especially respectful to guests in my home!"

Mrs. Silver Bear was not hiding her displeasure with Mr. Nuttybuddy. Silver Bear liked Mr. Nuttybuddy and probably put up with his complaining and brashness too much. Christmas Bear and Silver Bear watched in amusement as the squirrel cowered and said, "I'm sorry, Mrs. Silver Bear, I don't mean to be rude. I just don't understand how…"

Christmas Bear interrupted, "Mr. Nuttybuddy, the breach is good news because we expected it. It means we are anticipating our enemy's moves correctly and that is a good thing. Is there anything else you have for us?"

"No sir!" replied Mr. Nuttybuddy humbly.

"I think we should start for the lower fork," said Christmas Bear to Silver Bear. "Mr. Nuttybuddy, I would like you to tag along in case we need a messenger. Mrs. Silver Bear, if you would be so kind as to stay home in case we get any more messengers with news, I would appreciate it."

Mrs. Silver Bear saw them all to the door and watched as the two bears with the squirrel between them disappeared down the trail toward the Circle path.

Rebekah and Jonas came to a fork in the road that looked familiar to them.

"I think this is where we came up from our house and turned to go to Silver Bear's house," said Jonas. "I remember that rock."

"You're right," said Rebekah. "We have to turn right here to get home. We should be home in a few hours – if home is where it is supposed to be."

Jonas thought about getting home. "Dad's going to be mad," Jonas said. "We've been gone a long time. He's probably been looking for us for hours. You think we'll get it when we get home?"

Rebekah thought for a minute and said, "I don't think so. It wasn't like we ran off without telling him. We didn't ask to come here—we just ended up here. I think when we tell him what happened, he won't be mad. He's probably more worried than mad since we have never gone off like this before. I'm sure he thinks something bad has happened to us. That's why we need to get home as soon as we can. When he's sad and worried, he can act mad."

"Yeah," said Jonas thoughtfully. "I hope his worry and sadness turns to gladness when he sees us!"

Rebekah and Jonas turned right and started down the hill they came up to get to Treetop. They had traveled about twenty minutes when Jonas noticed that his breath didn't seem as frosty as it had been. He remembered what Silver Bear had told him about frosty breath being the sign of a good path, but he knew the farther he got from Treetop, the less frosty his breath would become.

"I wish our breath could always be frosty at home like it is here," said Jonas.

"Me, too" said Rebekah, "'But I'll trade frosty breath for home right now."

As they rounded a bend in the road, a light brown cougar that had been lying in the path got to his feet. The children stopped immediately at the sight of the cat.

"Don't be frightened," said the cougar. "Christmas Bear sent me. I have been waiting here to escort you the rest of the way home. You don't have far to go now, but there is need to be extra careful until your journey's end. Rustcoats have breached the southeast border of Treetop and their location is unknown at this time."

Rebekah relaxed a bit but was concerned about the news of the Rustcoats. "Do you think the Rustcoats have a good chance of finding us before we get home?"

"I don't think they do," said the cougar reassuringly. "Treetop is a big place, and they would have to be pretty fortunate to find you so quickly. If we hurry, you should be home long before they get through the east forest. The cougar turned to go down the hill and said, "Time is in our favor, so let's keep it that way and get moving."

The children followed the cougar down the path for several more minutes. He would turn his head back to look at them every so often, possibly giving them a cougar smile (they couldn't tell for sure), but he didn't say much. Soon they were approaching another fork in the road.

"Jonas!" said Rebekah excitedly, "that's the fork where we first met Silver Bear and Mr. Nuttybuddy, isn't it?"

Before Jonas could answer Rebekah, they both heard another loud snap of a dry twig breaking. This time it was off to their right and a bit in front of them. The brown cougar spun around at the noise. This time, the children didn't have to wonder about the source of the snap. A very mean looking black and grey cougar came walking out of the trees and positioned himself between the children and the brown cougar. The brown cougar made a start to get to Rebekah and Jonas, but the black and grey cougar blocked his way and let out a hideous scream that sent chills down their spines and stopped the brown cougar in its tracks.

"Twice in one day?" said the large cat to himself. "That's the second twig I have snapped today tracking you children." – not pleased with himself at all. Then the black and grey cougar said to Rebekah and Jonas menacingly, "You stay behind me! Don't even think about going over to that brown cat."

Skull heard the scream of the cougar off in the distance. "That would be Creeper," he said. "He has found the Children. Let's pick up the pace. Others could have heard him, too. We have to move fast now."

Skull, Stickers, and Weed began trotting toward the scream.

Christmas Bear, Silver Bear and Mr. Nuttybuddy heard a cougar scream as they walked down Treetop Path toward the downhill fork.

"That scream is coming from about where the children should be about now," said Christmas Bear. "We better hurry along."

Silver Bear didn't say anything as he and Christmas Bear took a left off the trail to short-cut through the forest toward the sound of the scream. Mr. Nuttybuddy climbed up a tree and began to speed through the treetops ahead of them.

Zeek heard a cougar scream off to his left in the distance. *That can't be good,* he said to himself. He wanted to run to the scream, but he knew he wouldn't be much help if it did mean trouble. "I've got to stay focused on my assignment," he whispered out loud as he picked up his already rapid pace to Silver Bear's house.

Whiskers heard a cougar scream while patrolling around Treetop Circle and immediately started running south to his friend's aid.

**Another Scolding**

# Chapter 21:

# Regret & Shame

S kippy and Jumper each took seven other rabbits with them to circle the Rustcoats and launch their rear assault. Skippy and his group had snuck about twenty feet behind what they thought was the last group of Rustcoats and were ready for the signal to start their diversion.

Jumper and his group had not yet reached the back line. A pack of about a dozen coyotes had decided to take a rest right in their path. They couldn't get around them without being noticed because the bush was too sparse in the immediate area.

"I don't like this," Jumper heard one of the coyotes say. "I think we should sneak back home. We were told this would be an easy trip and that we would be well fed along the way, but we haven't eaten anything since yesterday's lunch. It's been push, push, push to get here. I have a bad feeling about this whole deal."

"Yeah," said another coyote. "If they lied about the trip and the meals, what else have they lied about?"

"Oh, man!" exclaimed a third coyote, "What I wouldn't give for a nice fat juicy rabbit right about now."

The rest of the group all chimed in with "aaahhhs" and "mmmmms" at the thought of a rabbit supper.

Skippy and his rabbits thought they were in perfect position to launch their surprise run through the enemy ranks when another group of Rustcoats arrived at the battlefield behind them. These newcomers put them more toward the middle of their foes. The bush they were in was barely big enough to hide the eight of them. They only moved to it to launch their distraction assignment. It was not meant to be a hideout bush. They would surely be seen if an enemy got too close to them.

"Hurry up you slackers!" yelled someone who was obviously in charge. "Spread out, stay put, and be ready to move at once. You took your time getting here, so don't expect to get much of a rest!"

This lead wolf had come from the forward rebel ranks to "greet" the late arrivers. He stopped about ten feet in front of the bush where Skippy and his rabbits were positioned. Glancing around at his newest troops, he took notice of something shiny in the bush in front of him. It was the shine of rabbit eyes – Skippy's eyes. Skippy was looking right at Dameon, one of the wolves who had joined the Garden Rebellion centuries ago.

"Halt!" he shouted. The newcomers still moving stopped abruptly. The shouted order silenced the animals in the immediate area.

Skippy and his rabbits tensed. Dameon walked to within a few yards of the rabbit bush and crouched down. He sniffed the air and let out a low, menacing growl.

"What have we here?" he hissed. "It looks like…why, yes…it is. It's rabbits—rabbits hiding in **my** bush."

The Rustcoats closest to Dameon who heard his remarks began to squeal and sniff the air at the mention of rabbits. Soon the whole line heard something about rabbits being close by and they began to close in on Dameon. "Stay where you are!" Dameon ordered. They all stopped advancing, but the squealing and sniffing continued.

"Hmmmmm, rabbits with no scent. How peculiar." he said in a mocking tone. "What are you doing out here in the middle of all these hungry carnivores?" Dameon squinted at the rabbit bush and said, "Skippy, is that you, Skippy?"

Skippy needed time to think, so he stalled Dameon with questions.

"Dameon, I'm surprised to see you back here. What could you possibly be up to—except no good! What's with all the rabble with you?

Dameon growled. "Don't play dumb with me, Skippy! You think I'm stupid enough to believe we all surprised you and your buddies on your morning stroll?"

"Yes," said Skippy flatly, "I do think you're that stupid."

Dameon let out a menacing growl but made no move toward Skippy. He didn't want to start more of a commotion among his restless troops.

"You put yourself in the middle of trouble for a reason," snarled Dameon. "You better tell me why or you'll soon be somebody's breakfast."

Skippy figured this was a pretty good time to end his conversation with Dameon. He did the only thing he could think of doing under the circumstances. He screamed the rabbit death scream!

"Scatter towards home!" he shouted to the other rabbits.

All eight rabbits exploded out of the bush zigging and zagging in front of the surrounding Rustcoats.

Skippy headed right for Dameon. It was the last thing that Dameon expected as Skippy jumped, landed on the top of Dameon's head, and rebounded off—screaming all the way into the mass of Rustcoats between him and Treetop.

Dameon was furious and spun around to chase after Skippy. The Rustcoat troopers completely lost any pretense of order and scattered in all directions after the escaping rabbits.

Jumper heard Skippy scream. "They're in trouble! We've got to distract from here. Let's move!" yelled Jumper, and another eight rabbits plunged screaming into the startled group to Rustcoats in front of them. Another chase was on.

Hopper heard the rabbit scream coming from the battlefield. He knew Jumper and Skippy were in trouble. He immediately ran from cover and began to scream frantically and run back and forth before the Rustcoats on the frontline. Other rabbits followed Hopper's lead. They knew they had to draw the frontline Rustcoats after them now so Jumper and Skippy would have a better chance of getting their rabbits into the snake field.

The front line Rustcoats had just begun to head back to see what all the commotion behind them was about when the brush in front of them became alive with rabbits. They became focused on this immediate source of food and began to break ranks to help themselves to what they thought would be easy meals. Soon a major portion of the Rustcoat army was in turmoil.

Skippy, Jumper, and their rabbit squads had taken full advantage of the element of surprise. They'd quickly moved through the Rustcoats—back and forth, around and around, until they had the animals in their immediate area in a frenzy. Then they'd move to a new area of the camp with the frenzied animal in hot pursuit. The pursuing Rustcoats would tangle into the new group of Rustcoats as the new group began to join the pursuit after the darting rabbits. As the rabbits moved through the camp, the chaos following them grew larger and larger. Fights were erupting among the Rustcoats. They were tired and hungry, and they had lost all sense of order. The plan was working beautifully.

Stalker and his troops watched the enemy below as confusion erupted toward the rear of the Rustcoat mob. Then another disruption started on the south side of the enemy camp. From the hillside, these disruptions took on the appearance of waves. They rolled together in the middle and then spread rapidly to the front lines of the Rustcoats. The Rustcoats were entering Treetop as a wild mob—not as a trained army, just as the Treetoppers had hoped.

"One, two, three-four-five," said Winder as he counted the rabbits whizzing by him.

"Heeeere theeey come!" said Vennie who was coiled beside him.

"Don't bite until you hear Stalker howl," reminded Winder.

Winder and Vennie were engulfed in a mass of snarling, fighting, out-of-control Rustcoats. Dust was flying everywhere. They couldn't see more than ten feet in front of them in the confusion. All the snakes hunkered down to wait for the signal to attack as Rustcoats stumbled, rolled and ran past them.

At the east end of the snake field, Striker was watching the horde of Rustcoats rushing toward him as they carelessly chased the rabbits into the ambush prepared for them.

"They'll be here in a few minutes," Striker said to Slither. "Everything is going like clockwork."

Still farther up the hillside, Stalker and Pouncer were pleased with what they were watching. They had never seen such a beautiful mess. The rabbits had really done a job on the Rustcoats. They had completely disrupted the enemy invaders by running all through their ranks—building on the momentum of their confusion, anger, and hunger to draw them straight into the trap. Almost all the Rustcoats had crossed the border now and the lead intruders were almost at the base of the steeper part of the hill.

Pouncer looking down at the confusion below said, "It's just about time."

Stalker rose to his feet and watched as rabbits started spurting to safety from the mass of Rustcoats below him.

"I have counted only nineteen rabbits in the clear," said Stalker.

"Thirteen have already started up the hill. Ten more are clear to the north and are making their way here. Only one unaccounted..." Pouncer stopped in mid-sentence as a lone rabbit broke from the Rustcoats and headed up the hill. "That's twenty-four," said Pouncer. "They are now all out from among the Rustcoats."

Stalker immediately let out a piercing howl that was heard over the roar of battle below him. Stalker's howl was like no other – supernatural would be a good description of it. It got the attention of everyone on the battlefield.

Then the snakes struck.

From Pouncer's viewpoint, it looked like someone released dozens of coiled springs from the ground. The snakes struck the Rustcoats all over the battlefield. Yelps of pain and fear filled the air. Once bitten, a Rustcoat would try to back away from his attacker only to back into another. The Rustcoats who fled north or south on the battlefield were met by the stinging spray of the skunks and the needle-like spikes of the porcupines which drove them back into the snakes. The Rustcoats were forced to retreat west – the direction from which they had come. Most were limping, some were dragging themselves by their front legs in a desperate attempt to get away. Many lay on the field either dead or near death. The snake attack had devastated their ranks more than had been expected—and it all took no more than ten minutes.

Just as the snakes ended their attack and began heading back to Cedar Rest, the hornets moved in. The hornets were all over the Rustcoats in a matter of seconds. The Rustcoats were snapping at the air, spinning in circles, rolling on the ground, running into each other, desperately trying to escape the relentless swarms. The decimated invaders were slowly being driven into a crowded mass of wounded or dying animals on the western border of Treetop.

"Let's finish it," said Stalker coldly. "Stalker let out five short yipps, and all the Treetop warriors on the hillside with him rose to their feet.

Pouncer let out three loud bobcat screams. All the bobcats and wolverines on the north and south sides of the battlefield rose from their support positions in the brush and started to advance on the Rustcoats.

As the hornets broke off their attacks and headed back toward Treetop, the eagles and owls began their strafing operation. Their job was to keep the Rustcoats together near the border and to thwart all attempts to flee from Stalker as he led the advancing army of Treetoppers down the hillside.

The Rustcoats were trapped. They were being squeezed from all sides. The battle was coming to a victorious end for Treetop.

Dameon had seen the defeat coming as soon as the snakes struck his soldiers with such overwhelming force. He immediately hit the ground to play dead on the north side of the field. He laid there motionless until the battle noises dwindled to almost nothing. Then Dameon raised his head to peek over the bush he was laying by to see what was left of his army.

"So this is how a leader acts in battle—hiding behind a bush while his troops get massacred?"

Dameon jerked his head to his right to see who chided him. He froze when he saw the large rattlesnake coiled three feet from his face. He recognized the snake. "Vennie," said Dameon flatly.

"We were coming for you, Dameon. We saw you go down pretending to be dead."

"Who's 'we'?" asked Dameon, not taking his eyes off the snake.

Vennie nodded toward Winder's position in a bush to Dameon's left.

Dameon's eyes darted to the brush and saw Winder poised to strike.

"We didn't see Skull anywhere, Dameon," said Vennie in a slightly mocking tone. "Does he now send play-dead wolves to do his fighting for him?"

Dameon glared at Vennie, but he didn't dare move. He said nothing.

"Where is Skull?" asked Vennie coldly.

"I wouldn't tell you if I knew," said Dameon defiantly.

"Then you are of no use to us."

Dameon saw Winder spring at him out of the corner of his eye, but he wasn't fast enough to get out of the way. Winder bit him on the side of the neck. Dameon jerked to his feet. The bite burned so badly that he could hardly take a breath. Dameon shook his head as if trying to shake the poison from his body. Then Vennie stuck Dameon in the throat just under his mouth. The burning got worse. Dameon stumbled a few steps and fell to the ground. Breathing became harder. Then he could no longer see anything.

Dameon was terrified. He hadn't been this fearful since The Fall. As he struggled for breath, he found himself thinking thoughts that he had always refused to dwell on. He was regretting his association with Skull. He had hated Skull's arrogance, he had hated how he mistreated everyone around him, and he despised himself for allowing Skull to get away with it all. He had known he was the only wolf who could have possibly ended Skull's reign of terror, and he had done nothing. Another new emotion flooded his mind–he was ashamed of himself. He was dying, and his last feeling was shame.

Waiting for his agony to end seemed an eternity to him. Dameon's death throes lasted only a few minutes; then he was just another body in a sea of bodies on the battlefield.

## Chapter 22:

# Bad News Is Good News—Again

Z eek ran up to the front door of Silver Bear's house and let out a chatter that would have awakened a bear in hibernation. Mrs. Silver Bear answered the door, and Zeek wasted no time on pleasantries.

"I saw Skull, Stickers and Weed in east Treetop. They are headed for some path…I don't know which path…and Creeper's with them….I mean Creeper came with them but wasn't with them when I saw them…I mean…"

"Calm down, dear. I can barely keep up with you talking so fast."

"Please, Mrs. Silver Bear, I've got to talk with Christmas Bear and Silver Bear," pleaded Zeek.

"Indeed you do. Fortunately, they have left already."

Zeek looked at her in disbelief, "Fortunately…they left already?" he said a bit confused.

"Yes, Zeek, I believe they left for the path you are referring to—that's what is fortunate," Mrs. Silver Bear said pleasantly. "But let's go there to make sure. I don't want to be guessing on a matter as serious as this."

Mrs. Silver Bear closed the door behind her and stood next to Zeek. "Climb up on my back. I know the most direct route to the path, and you look so awfully tired."

An exhausted, but grateful Zeek hopped up on Mrs. Silver Bear's back, and off she ran into the forest.

The two cougars glared and growled at each other as Rebekah and Jonas slowly backed up the path. They got behind a large pine and peaked around the trunk to watch the standoff. The black and grey cougar was about fifteen yards away now, and the brown cougar was another twenty yards down from there. The black and grey cougar had seen them backing away, so he backed up a few steps in their direction.

"Children," said the brown cougar. "Try to circle around and get behind me. Grab a dead branch or some rocks to protect yourself. If he tries to stop you, I'll intervene. Do what I tell you, now!"

The children started to look around for branches and rocks.

"Don't listen to him," said the black and grey cougar. "He means you harm, not good."

"Children, that cat doesn't want you to get home. He's your enemy, not your friend," warned the brown cougar. "You know time is important, and you know this is the way to your house. He is purposely delaying you from going home. He has been following you like a sneak. A friend doesn't do that. I waited for you in the open on the road. If I meant you harm, I wouldn't have done that. I would have snuck up on you—just like he did."

The brown cougar made sense and Rebekah and Jonas continued to look for weapons as they made their way into the forest to the left of the black and grey cougar.

The black and grey cougar let out a growl that gave Rebekah and Jonas goose bumps. The black and grey cat paced back and forth a few times and said to himself, "Very well, let's try this."

The black and grey cougar got low to the ground and made a giant leap toward the children. The move startled them and as they turned to run, they stumbled into each other and fell to the ground at the foot of the tree. The black and grey cat pounced next to them and warned in a hoarse whisper, "Don't either of you move a muscle."

The brown cougar started to advance on the black and grey cougar,

148

but the black and grey cougar turned his head toward him and said, "You come any closer—I'll kill you."

Rebekah and Jonas were scared. The brown cougar looked tough, but the black and grey cougar looked meaner. His green eyes were fierce. The brown cougar stopped coming toward them. Rebekah and Jonas didn't think the brown cougar was going to be able to help them.

In the middle of all this confusion and danger, Jonas looked at Rebekah and pointed to his nose.

Rebekah whispered frantically, "I know, Jonas, this situation stinks, but I don't know what to do!"

Jonas raised his eyebrows, pointed to his nose, and nodded toward the black and grey cougar.

Rebekah looked at Jonas like he was crazy. "What is wrong with you?" she whispered loudly.

Jonas leaned over and whispered in Rebekah's ear, "Pine scent. This cougar has the pine scent."

Rebekah's eyes got wide. She bent over and took a sniff of the black and grey cougar fur. He definitely had the pine scent.

"My name is Shadow. Christmas Bear sent me to watch over your journey home. Whatever I tell you to do, you must do without hesitation – understood?" Shadow didn't wait for an answer. "Good! Now I need you to climb this tree. Do it now!"

Rebekah and Jonas looked at the tree. It was a wide tree, but it had coarse bark and a few small, low branches that could hold their weight. They started their climb immediately and reached the larger branches about fifteen feet off the ground. . They had just settled on the lowest, high branch when they heard noises from the forest behind the brown cougar.

Skull, Stickers, and Weed emerged from the trees.

Skull came up beside the brown cougar and glared at Shadow for a moment before he asked, "Where's the children, Creeper?"

"They're in the tree by Shadow."

Skull looked in the tree and saw the children in the branches. He then turned his attention to Shadow.

"You can't take the four of us, Shadow?" said Skull scornfully.

"I don't have to take the four of you. The two cowards behind you won't be much help to you, and Creeper is the only one who can reach the Children." Shadow looked at Creeper. "So, Creeper, if any of your friends here pick a fight, my attention will be on you alone."

Creeper didn't show it, but he was scared. He knew Shadow wasn't bluffing, and he also knew that he was no match for this Treetop warrior.

Stickers and Weed resented being called cowards. They both growled ferociously. However, both wolves were still several feet behind Skull and Creeper, and they made no attempt to join them.

"Stickers, Weed, I want you to start moving around behind Shadow," ordered Skull. "Creeper, stay close to me. We'll fight Shadow together."

Stickers and Weed began to do as they were told. Shadow turned and in one leap was in the branches next to the children—looking down on his foes. "You can position your gang anywhere you like, but Creeper is the only one who can reach us. Creeper, you'll have to take me on all by yourself."

"What are we going to do now?" asked Stickers.

**Last Obstacle**

# Chapter 23:

# Wreaths to Treetop Circle

Stalker looked over the bodies strewn all over the battlefield. The Rustcoat army was completely destroyed. Stalker had dismissed most of the Treetoppers to Cedar Rest, but he asked Talon and Bomber to remain for a meeting with Striker and his snake lieutenants.

"You all did superbly in battle," said Stalker, "especially you and your snakes, Striker."

"Thank you, Stalker, but the real heroes today were Hopper and his crew," said Striker humbly. "They organized and executed a brilliant plan in battle conditions."

"Thank you for saying so, Striker. I will convey your praise of Hopper and his rabbits to Christmas Bear. I am sure he will commend you both for your actions, but now I must turn our attention to the children. As you all know, Dameon was the only Rustcoat leader of note in this battle. That means Skull is somewhere else doing his evil business. I figure he is leading a group to capture the children himself. I want to send more help to Shadow in case he needs it."

"What do you have in mind?" asked Talon.

"I would like you and Bomber to bring Striker, Vennie, Slither, and Winder to Shadow immediately. The children should be somewhere on the path south of Treetop Circle by now. Find them. Shadow will be trailing them in the Pines, so he might not be visible. You should be able to find the children quickly from the air."

Stalker turned to Striker and said, "I know you all hate flying, but I don't see how else we can do this in time to be of help if we are needed."

Striker sighed. "I don't disagree with your plan. It makes sense and we'll do it, but let's do it quickly so we don't have to think about it much."

Talon actually looked like he might have been smiling. "You and Vennie can come with me," he said to Striker. "Bomber will take Slither and Winder."

"And Pouncer and I will be following you up the switchbacks from the battlefield," said Stalker.

Talon instructed the snakes to pair up and tangle themselves in a loose knot. He and Bomber gently wrapped their talons around the snakes and took off looking for the children. The eagles looked like they were carrying wreaths to Treetop Circle.

"You think there's a good chance for more trouble?" asked Pouncer.

"I think there will be trouble, and I want my best assassins in position to take care of it," said Stalker.

**Eagle Wreaths**

Skull was glaring at Shadow in the tree next to Rebekah and Jonas. There was a low growl in his throat. He knew time was not on his side. He had to get the children quickly before any more Treetoppers showed up, but that did not look very likely. He knew Shadow was a fierce warrior and that Creeper was no match for him. While all this was swirling in his head, Creeper interrupted his thoughts with the same question Stickers had bothered him with a few minutes ago,

"What are we going to do?" asked Creeper.

"You're going to **die**, that's what **you're** going to do," said a familiar voice.

Everyone turned to see Mr. Nuttybuddy high in a tree across the road from the one Shadow, Rebekah and Jonas were in. "You all made a fatal mistake coming back to Treetop uninvited."

"We got to get out of here," said Weed. "First Shadow…now that busybody Nuttybuddy—who else is going to show up here, Skull? I thought you said we would get in and get out."

"Shut-up!" snapped Skull. Skull was scanning the forest around them slowly and carefully. His ears were turning every which way trying to pick up the sound of more approaching Treetoppers.

"Looking for us?" said another familiar voice.

Everyone except Mr. Nuttybuddy looked to see who else had joined their standoff. It was Christmas Bear and Silver Bear.

"It's unfortunate for you, Skull, that you continue to overestimate your abilities. But that is just what a fool does, isn't it Skull?" said Christmas Bear?

"And you," said Christmas Bear, looking at Creeper, Stickers, and Weed in turn, "You follow an evil fool, and you will share his fate."

Sticker, Weed, and Creeper began to back away from Skull. Skull glanced back at them and was going to say something to them, but instead just looked at them in disgust and turned back to face Christmas Bear.

The three cowardly Rustcoats continued to back away from Skull and were about to make a break for the forest when they heard a chirping sound off to their right. It was Zeek, and he was low enough on the tree for them to get him. Weed made a move toward Zeek—and it turned out to be his last.

Mrs. Silver Bear was finally able to give Weed a piece of her paw. She struck him with such force that he went flying into the tree Zeek was on. Zeek had to scramble out of the way as Weed struck the tree where he had been clinging. Weed squealed once and slid limply down the trunk to the ground.

Mrs. Silver Bear moved quickly to block the roads south and west at the fork. Silver Bear moved to keep the remaining Rustcoats from retreating east. Christmas Bear remained where he was blocking the path to Treetop Circle. And to make matters worse for the intruders, Whiskers walked out of the trees just below the tree Shadow and the children were in.

Stickers and Creeper were startled by Mrs. Silver Bear's attack and looked to Skull for what to do next, but Skull was nowhere in sight. In the commotion of the attack on Weed, he had bolted to the fork in the road and had headed west before Mrs. Silver Bear had blocked that way of escape.

Talon and Bomber spotted a group of creatures near a fork in the road below them. One creature had just bolted from the main road and was running down the west fork.

"Hmmm," said Bomber, "Looks like we got here just in time."

"It looks like someone is in a really big hurry," answered Talon. "I'll follow the runner. You go down and see what the creatures at the fork are up to."

"Right," said Bomber as he started his descent.

Talon made a wide turn and headed back west to follow the running black wolf.

Creeper and Stickers were tail to tail, Creeper was keeping an eye on Shadow and Whiskers while Stickers tried to keep track of the bears. Nobody had said anything since Mrs. Silver Bear finished off Weed. Rebekah and Jonas were feeling pretty safe now with all the Treetoppers around.

"We just want to get out of here," Stickers said to anyone who was listening. "Skull planned this whole thing and he's run off. As far as I'm concerned, this is over. Just let us go; there is no need for a fight."

"Skull planned this whole thing?" repeated Christmas Bear. "What was his plan? Why did you sneak back here?" he inquired.

"Because Skull..."

Creeper interrupted Stickers by bumping him, and he glared at Stickers as he said, "We were told that since the humans were let back in the Garden, we would be welcome back also. We were told that the loving God you serve finally decided to forgive us for being just like he made us," Creeper said – seething with bitterness.

Silver Bear asked Stickers, "Is what Creeper says true, Stickers? Did you think the children were a good sign for you?"

"Yeah, that's right. We thought we would be welcomed back. Forgiveness was what we expected. Yeah, Creeper's right."

"If you expected to be welcomed because of the children, why did you try to harm them when they first entered Treetop?" countered Silver Bear.

Whiskers added, "If you thought you would be welcomed back, why did you sneak into Treetop in the dark while your army marched to the field below Cedar Rest?"

Creeper and Stickers were tangled in their lies, but being the fool that he was, Stickers figured he could lie his way out of his lie.

"I didn't try to harm the children," said Stickers slyly. "It was the mortal Rustcoats who attacked the Children."

Christmas Bear addressed Stickers, "You think half the truth is the truth, Stickers? The truth is that you are a liar. You have ignorant animals do your dirty work and then try to play innocent. You are despicable."

"And you," Christmas Bear looked at Creeper, "You talk about forgiveness like you deserve it. You blame God for the evil that you do and expect us to believe you came here thinking God would welcome you back? God will not be mocked, Creeper! This is the end of you. Here. Now."

At that moment, Bomber swooped next to Christmas Bear and hovered a few inches off the ground.

"You two can open your eyes now," Bomber said to Slither and Winder. "I'm going to let you down."

The two snakes hit the ground, unknotted themselves and immediately began to slowly glide toward Creeper and Stickers.

**A Fatal Mistake**

# Chapter 24:

# Unhappy Reunion

S kull had slowed his pace to a trot as he fled westward. He was
furious his plan to capture the children had failed, and that failure
re-energized his hatred for his Treetop enemies. He knew he would be
pursued. He also knew his present state of mind could be a problem
for him.

*Dameon often told me my bad temper caused me to make mistakes –
like running down the middle of this path instead of concealing myself in
the trees. I've got to get control of this rage.*

Skull approached a series of switchbacks that steeply declined down
the mountainside. He wanted to find his army and wreak havoc in
Treetop. The thought of revenge began to calm him a bit, so he stopped
for a moment to think about what he was doing. There he decided that
going down the mountain across the switchbacks would give him better
concealment than following their paths all the way down. He was just
about to execute this plan when he heard voices on the road below him.
He quickly jumped from the road and hid in some thick bushes next
to a huge rock.

Talon had been watching as Skull hid from the approaching
Treetoppers. Stalker and Pouncer were about a hundred yards from
the end of the switchback. That put them almost right below where
Skull had hidden himself.

"You guys watching this," ask Talon.

"Yes," said Striker. "I see him. Put us down in the forest behind where he's hiding. We can move in on him while his attention is on Stalker and Pouncer."

Talon made a wide turn and swung around behind Skull and dropped the snakes off in the forest.

"The Rustcoat animals were defeated easier than I thought they would be," Pouncer was saying.

"They had little leadership on the battlefield," said Stalker. "Skull and some of his lieutenants have to be up to mischief somewhere else in Treetop. This battle was too crucial for them not to be a part of it."

Skull couldn't hear any more of the conversation because the Treetoppers had moved past him toward the top of the switchback. He growled to himself as he pondered the news of his army's swift defeat. With their defeat at the border of Treetop, he now had no chance to keep the children from returning home. His rage flared up again.

As he was fuming, Skull looked to the sky and caught a glimpse of an eagle disappearing in the treetops north of his hiding place. The eagle appeared to be carrying his dinner. That was not unusual in Rustcoat, but in Treetop—that sight was not normal. Treetop animals don't eat each other; they eat a green substance called Heaven's Grain. Skull thought about what the eagle might be carrying for a moment, but his mind returned to the conversation he overheard about his army losing their battle. Meanwhile, the two close Treetoppers climbed the last switchback and were now on level ground heading east.

"Stop!" whispered Stalker insistently. Pouncer froze in his tracks. Stalker sniffed the air. He took a few steps and sniffed some more. He stood there for over a minute listening and sniffing.

Pouncer was looking everywhere and sniffing the air, too, but couldn't pick up anything. Then Stalker whispered to Pouncer, "There's a Rustcoat animal somewhere nearby. I only got a brief scent, but I'm sure of it."

"Let's get off the road quietly and hide ourselves among the trees for a bit. We'll just sit and listen for a while," said Pouncer.

The two of them moved off the road and hid themselves by some rocks and trees nearby.

Skull was becoming restless. The voices he had heard were on the road right below him and close enough so that whoever was talking should have passed him by now. *Where did they go?* Shull thought to himself as he inched his way out of his hiding place to get a glimpse of the road.

"There, over there," whispered Pouncer. "See by that big sloping rock over there—at the bottom—someone's peeking out."

Sure enough, half a face appeared at the base of the rock—enough for an eye to see the road.

"It's Skull," whispered Stalker as he stood up from where he was laying.

The head immediately shot back behind the rock.

"Skull!" shouted Stalker as he walked toward the rock Skull was hiding behind. "I saw you duck back behind the rock so there is no sense in hiding anymore." Stalker walked to within thirty feet of where Skull had disappeared.

Skull closed his eyes and tried to think of how he might get away from Stalker–but came up with nothing. Stalker had been his closest friend before the rebellion. *Of all the wolves for me to meet like this, why did it have to be Stalker!*

Skull sighed, opened his eyes, and walked out from behind the rock. He faced Stalker standing in the road.

"Well," said Skull, "now what happens?"

Stalker couldn't answer right away. Seeing his old friend tugged at his heart. He had fond memories of him and Skull before the rebellion–Scully was his name back then. Stalker felt an strong pull to be lenient with him, but he knew that was impossible at this point. Skull was an enemy of God and therefore his enemy, too. He silently prayed that God would give him the strength to do whatever he was supposed to do, but he couldn't deny that he didn't want to hurt Skull.

"Why did you have to come back?" asked Stalker sadly. "Why didn't you just stay away as you were told?"

"How would that have changed things," asked Skull showing no emotion. "After the children were home safely, you would have just come after us in Rustcoat. Rustcoat—here—what difference does it make where this happens?"

"You're right," said Stalker. "This was going to happen sooner or later, so why go after the children? They were just the messengers signifying the beginning of the end for you. Capturing them would not have changed your fate."

"It may not have changed it, but it could have delayed it," answered Skull.

"You still don't get it," said Stalker. "You can't alter God's plan by anything you do. Using your reasoning, I could argue that you have caused your troubles to come on you sooner than they would have. I could say, 'If you had stayed away, we would have had to take the time to find you. Since you came to us, your feared end has come sooner.' You have fought God's plan from the beginning, and His plan is unalterable."

"Then it doesn't really make much difference what we do, does it Stalker?" said Skull with defiance beginning to show in his voice. "We're just puppets for Him to play with, aren't we? He makes us like we are and then punishes or rewards us for how He made us. What kind of God does that?" asked Skull with contempt.

"It is not our place to question our Maker," said Stalker flatly. "You think you are God's judge? That things should go according to Skull's will?" said Stalker with a little impatience now showing in his voice. "You're crazy, Skull. There is no simpler way to put it. You've created nothing yet you judge creation and the creator. Your mind is bent, and whether you bent it or He bent it makes no difference to those of us who have to deal with the likes of you. We still have to live with the consequences of your sinful behavior here and now."

"We've had this argument before," said Skull. "Funny how such disagreements can separate friends, family…" Skull's voice trailed off.

"There is nothing funny about it," said Stalker with emotion starting to creep back in his voice.

The two wolves stood there looking at each other for a few moments.

"I ask again," said Skull. "What happens now?"

Stalker stared at Skull. He didn't know what to say.

Pouncer got up from his hiding place and began to approach Stalker.

"Oh, so that's who you were talking with earlier," said Skull. "I had forgotten all about him."

As Pouncer walked toward Stalker, Talon flew in from north of the switchbacks and landed on a branch of a pine between Stalker and Skull.

"Talon," said Skull looking up, "where's that package you were carrying? That was you in the sky a while ago, wasn't it? I was wondering if that package was your dinner," said Skull sarcastically.

"Hello, Skull. I wish our reunion could have been under more pleasant circumstances," said Talon sincerely.

Skull checked the ground around him as best he could while facing Talon. "So, where are they?"

"Behind you."

Skull glanced back and saw the two rattlers about ten feet behind him. He stared at them for a moment and then looked at Stalker. Stalker had now been joined by Pouncer.

"You and your friends going to beat me up?" asked Skull mockingly as he looked at Stalker. "No fair fight for an old friend?"

Stalker just stared at Skull–his eyes tearing up.

Skull glanced at Pouncer—then at Talon. "You two I would fight," he said. "But I can't fight my old friend." Skull looked at Stalker and smiled ever so slightly. Then he turned to face the snakes.

"Snakes," said Skull scornfully. "They helped start this whole mess, and now they help finish it. God does have a sense of balance, doesn't he?"

Defiant to the last, Skull charged the snakes. He was so quick that he was over the snakes before they had a chance to coil and strike. Stalker tensed but before he could move, Skull stopped his attack. Striker and Vennie coiled and struck Skull in the chest just behind his front legs and scurried out from beneath him to get ready for a second attack.

Skull just stood there, facing away from the stunned Treetoppers. His head was down, his breathing was becoming labored, but he made no other sound—not even when he was bitten.

The poison was potent. Skull could feel it travelling to his heart. It burned so badly. He couldn't take a deep breath. He was becoming dizzy, and his front legs collapsed under him. His back legs then collapsed and he fell on his side. He looked up at Talon in the tree, but Talon had his head down and was not looking at him. Everything then got blurry and the burning pain turned to a freezing cold, and then it was over.

Talon flew down to the snakes and motioned for them to get ready to leave. They knotted themselves and Talon gathered them in his claws.

"Thank you," said Stalker, showing emotion that none of the Treetoppers had ever seen before. "I couldn't have…"

"Yes you could have," said Talon. "I was watching you. You could have, but the Lord is merciful."

# Chapter 25:

# A Far Away Voice

C reeper was not going to tangle with poisonous snakes. He would rather take his chances fighting with the other Treetoppers who surrounded him. Before the snakes could get within striking distance, Creeper lunged toward the tree the Children were in and then leaped for Rebekah and Jonas. Shadow immediately reacted and hit Creeper in the air just before he reached Jonas. Jonas flinched back, lost his balance, and fell out of the tree.

Rebekah screamed, "Jonas!"

The stand-off turned into a ruckus. The two cougars were fighting; Stickers attempted to flee but Silver Bear blocked his escape and drove him back to the snakes; the snakes bit Stickers and he was yelping so loudly it hurt Rebekah's ears; and Zeek and Mr. Nuttybuddy were chattering up a storm. Rebekah tried to look where Jonas has fallen, but she almost fell trying to turn on the branch. Then all the skirmishes seemed to end a once, and there was quiet.

Shadow stood panting over the motionless body of Creeper. Stickers lie dead in the middle of the road from the snake bites. Mrs. Silver Bear and Christmas Bear had run to the spot where Jonas had fallen from the tree. Rebekah finally managed to get herself turned around and looked down to see if Jonas was ok.

"Where'd he go? Where's Jonas?" Rebekah asked in a panicky voice.

Christmas Bear and Mrs. Silver Bear were looking around the trees and bushes nearby. Silver Bear and Shadow came over to the tree to help.

"Where did Jonas go?" asked Rebekah for the third time.

No one said anything for a while. Then Christmas Bear looked up to Rebekah and said, "I think he's home. Yes, I believe that's where he must be."

Ding ding ding ding ding.

Jonas sat up on the sit-rock. For a moment he didn't know where he was. Then he saw his brother, Daniel, by the house ringing the "come in" bell.

"Come on, you two, time for breakfast," called Daniel.

"Home—how could he be home? He was just here! He just fell out of the tree!" said Rebekah excitedly.

"Well, I can't explain it myself, but that's where I think he is," said Christmas Bear. "He must have completed his assignment, and he was allowed to go home."

"What about me?" asked Rebekah as she was helped down from the tree. "I like you guys and all, but I want to be with my brother. I want to go home, too."

"Oh, you will go home," said Christmas Bear, "but I guess your assignment isn't quite finished yet."

"What do I have to do to finish it," asked Rebekah anxiously. "If Jonas gets back home and I'm not with him, everyone's going to be worried sick! What do I have to do? What do I have to do?"

"You must be patient, Rebekah. You must always remember to trust in the Lord. When he's finished with you here, you will be home," advised Christmas Bear. "All things are in his hands, and you needn't worry about outcomes. It always works out just the way He planned it.

"Rebekah! Rebekah!"

Rebekah could hear Jonas calling her, but she couldn't tell where he was calling from. He sounded far away.

"There," said Christmas Bear, "Jonas isn't as far away from you as you thought. Can't you hear him?" Christmas Bear looked at Rebekah and smiled.

Rebekah felt strange – like part of her was missing. It was hard to put into words. She looked over at Silver Bear.

"Silver Bear, thank you so much for saving us from the wolves, and thank you for showing us the way to Christmas Bear."

"It was an honor to serve you, Rebekah," said Silver Bear, bowing his head to her.

"Mrs. Silver Bear, I don't think Jonas and I thanked you enough for your hospitality. We loved your home and enjoyed the food you gave us."

"I know you are grateful, Rebekah," said Mrs. Silver Bear, "but thank you for mentioning it. May the Lord allow you to visit us again."

"Shadow, you stood alone against those Rustcoats and saved Jonas and I. For that we will be forever thankful," said Rebekah.

"I am glad I was able to help you, Rebekah," said Shadow. "I hope God allows you to be with your brother soon."

Rebekah looked up into the trees and found where Mr. Nuttybuddy and Zeek were sitting. "I want to thank you two for all the help you gave us behind the scenes. You are every bit as much warriors as those with big teeth and claws."

Mr. Nuttybuddy turned to Zeek with his chest out and said, "I knew all along these kids were alright...probably only live on the outskirts of Rustcoat."

Zeek just looked at Mr. Nuttybuddy, smiled and shook his head in bewilderment.

Rebekah turned to Christmas Bear and said, "I wish I could tell Talon, Stalker, and Striker how grateful I am for their help."

"You just did," smiled Christmas Bear. "We are thankful that God chose you and Jonas to come to us. God always picks the perfect people for the job He needs done. I'm glad he picked you two."

"Rebekah!" called Jonas again—only this time it was closer and louder.

Christmas Bear was giving her a very warm smile as he vanished before her eyes and, in his place, Rebekah saw Jonas looking down at her.

"Come on, Rebekah!" said Jonas, "Daniel said it's breakfast time."

Rebekah sat up and just looked around her for a moment. She was on the sit-rock. Her house was where it was supposed to be. Jonas was on the sit-rock next to her. She looked back at the rock fort and started to get up.

"I already checked," said Jonas knowingly. "Our rock fort is like it's supposed to be, too.

Rebekah looked at Jonas with astonishment. "Jonas, did you...did we...?"

"I think we had the same dream," offered Jonas.

"How do you know we had the same dream?"

"I heard you talking in your sleep before you woke up," answered Jonas. You were saying good-bye to all the animals in my dream, so we must have had the same dream."

"Whoa," said Rebekah, "how can that be?"

"I don't know," said Jonas, "but Christmas Bear, Silver Bear and Mrs. Silver Bear, Mr. Nutty..."

"They were all in your dream, too!" said Rebekah in amazement. "Jonas, how did you get back here?" asked Rebekah excitedly.

"The last thing I remember was Creeper jumping at me and Shadow smashing into him midair. Then I fell from the tree and heard bells," Daniel was ringing the 'come in' bell and calling us to breakfast."

"I was there. I saw the same things! I saw you fall from the tree!"

They both sat there for a few moments in silence. "This is weird. How could we have the exact same dream?" asked Rebekah.

Daniel called again, "Hey, you two, get down here for breakfast! Everyone's waiting!"

## Chapter 26:

# More than Strange

Rebekah and Jonas climbed down the sit-rock and ran down the hill to the house. They burst through the kitchen door and both started talking at once.

"Damom, webekah hadtbame dabream christreebarop," said Rebekah and Jonas speaking over one another.

"Don't talk at the same time," scolded Dad. "And don't burst in here talking without first waiting to see if you might be interrupting anyone."

"Sorry, Daddy," said Rebekah as she started toward her seat at the table.

"Daddy, we had a dream about Christmas Bear," said Rebekah.

"Mom, Rebekah and I had the same dream," added Jonas.

"Both of you go wash your hands and come back to the table before the food gets cold. Then you can tell us all about your dreams," said Mom.

Rebekah and Jonas went to the bathroom to wash their hands while Mom and Sarah, their older sister, put the scones on the table and the ham and eggs on each plate. When Jonas put his hands under the water, he noticed that the cuff on his jacket was torn off.

"Rebekah!" Jonas exclaimed, "I forgot about my sleeve!"

Rebekah looked at his sleeve and remembered how it had gotten torn in their dream.

"My jacket was torn by some bad wolves in my dream. When we went up there this morning to have cocoa, it wasn't torn. We were just sitting on the rock" said Jonas, looking for some other explanation from Rebekah.

"I remember the wolves tearing your coat when I pulled you into the rock cave."

Jonas looked at Rebekah, "If you tear your jacket in a dream, it doesn't end up torn in real life. If we were just dreaming, how did I tear my jacket?"

"If you two don't get in here you're going to get it," shouted Dad from the kitchen.

Rebekah and Jonas quickly finished washing their hands and headed back to the kitchen.

"What am I going to tell mom about the jacket?" whispered Jonas.

"Take it off for now until I can think…"

"Tell me what about your jacket," asked mom as she met them in the hall to hurry them to the table. "Oh, Jonas! What did you do to your sleeve? Your cuff's completely torn off?"

Jonas replied, "I….I…."

"Never mind now," said Mom, "get to the breakfast table so we can all eat."

Rebekah and Jonas took their places at the table, Dad thanked God for the food, and everyone but Rebekah and Jonas began to eat.

"So, what's this about you and Jonas having the same dream about Christmas Bear?" asked Dad.

"First, I would like to know how you tore your jacket, Jonas," interjected Mom.

Jonas looked at his mom and then his dad. Mom and Dad were both looking at him for an answer.

"Well," said Jonas. "I'm not sure exactly how it happened."

"How could you not be sure how a tear like that happened?" asked Mom. "Your whole cuff is torn off. You would know how that happened," she insisted.

"It happened in our dream," blurted out Rebekah.

Dad looked up from his ham and eggs and gave Rebekah one of his "looks."

John, Rebekah's eldest brother, said, "Nice try, Rebekah. I never tried that excuse before."

"Dreams aren't real and jackets don't get torn in them," said Mom.

"I don't know how I tore it," said Jonas, "but in my dream it did get torn."

"OK," said Dad a little amused, "tell us how it got torn in your dream."

Jonas related how he and Rebekah were on the sit-rock when wolves came up the driveway and chased them into the rock fort—or rock cave as it turned out. He explained the tug-of-war he, Rebekah and a wolf had at the cave entrance where the wolf tore off his cuff.

"And you had the same dream, Rebekah?" asked Dad.

"Yes. The same one."

"Exactly the same one?" questioned Dad.

"Exactly the same one. I know it sounds goofy, but it was exactly the same one!" insisted Rebekah.

Dad looked at Rebekah and Jonas and said, "I think you might have had more like a daydream. It sounds like you both might have had my Christmas Bear story in the back of your minds as you were pretending that wolves were chasing after you. The jacket must have gotten torn while you were fooling around in the rock fort."

"It was different from a daydream, Daddy," offered Rebekah. "I can't explain it, but it was different."

"After breakfast, you two go back to the rock fort and look around for that cuff," ordered Mom. "I can sew it back on so you can get more use out of that Jacket."

"Yes, Mama," said Rebekah and Jonas.

"I'll go up with you after breakfast and help you look for it," said Daniel.

As they finished their breakfast, Rebekah and Jonas told everyone the rest of the dream they had. What was odd was that Rebekah would start telling a portion of her dream and Jonas would finish telling it with what was in his dream. Then Jonas would tell a portion of his dream and Rebekah would do the same thing—finishing off his story. The details of the dreams were amazingly coherent—not like most dreams that are a bunch of odd, disconnected scenes.

"Your dream would make a good story," said Daniel to Rebekah and Jonas. "You should write it down, Dad. I've never considered how the animals felt or what they were like in the Garden during and after the fall. The more I think about it, the more fascinated I become about the wonder of it."

"It's the best dream or daydream I've ever heard," admitted Dad. "Maybe I will put it in their kid books so we don't forget it."

When breakfast was finished, Dad, Daniel, Rebekah and Jonas headed up to the sit-rock. On their way, Rebekah and Jonas relived for them the wolves coming up the drive, how the fog creeped up the drive and engulfed them, and how the rock fort ended up looking like a jumble of rocks that formed a rock cave.

They all stopped at the sit-rock and looked around for Jonas' jacket cuff. Rebekah and Jonas looked for it, but they didn't expect to find it. They couldn't explain it, but somehow their dream was real. The cuff was in Treetop—not here.

"I don't see it here," said Dad, "Let's check out the rock fort. You may have torn your jacket climbing around on the rocks there."

Rebekah, Jonas and Dad entered the rock fort and began to look around for the cuff. Daniel walked past the rock fort entrance and climbed up on the rocks east of the fort to sit and enjoy the cool morning. As he was getting comfortable, he looked toward the hill behind their property. He saw something out of place next to the huge bell-shaped rock just beyond their fence line. At first he thought it was some kind of cat sitting up there, but on closer inspection, it turned out to be a very large bird.

"Dad," Daniel whispered, "come here for a second."

Dad left Rebekah and Jonas in the fort and came around to where Daniel was sitting.

"Look at that," said Daniel pointing to the bell-shaped rock.

Dad looked and saw the bird on the ledge next to the bell rock. He stared at the bird for a few moments and said, "That looks like an eagle—the biggest Eagle I have ever seen. I've never seen one quite like that around here before. Boy, it's a big one!"

Rebekah and Jonas heard Dad say something about a "big one" and climbed up the east side of the rock fort to take a look. As they got next to Daniel, they also saw the bird. He was mostly black with a scatter of grey on his breast. He was beautiful and menacing at the same time.

Rebekah and Jonas looked at each other with a combination of disbelief and awe.

"It looks like he's got part of an animal in his mouth," said Daniel. "I wish I had our binoculars."

The eagle let out a loud screech.

"Let's be quiet so we don't scare him off. I want to watch him for a while," said Dad.

They all sat or stood on the east side of the rock fort looking at the eagle. The eagle remained next to the bell rock—seemingly staring back at them. Suddenly, a smaller animal emerged from behind the eagle and stopped at the eagle's feet.

**An Unexpected Visit**

"That stupid squirrel!" said Dad. "He's going to be that eagle's breakfast."

Dad said the squirrel must have climbed up the jumble of rocks behind the bell rock and mistakenly came out where the eagle was standing, but the squirrel didn't move from the eagle's feet. The eagle just looked down at the squirrel but made no move toward it. After a few moments, the eagle dropped what was in his mouth and it fell by the squirrel. Still the squirrel didn't move.

"If you don't want to watch a squirrel getting "ate," I suggest you turn your heads," said Dad. "The eagle has dropped whatever it was planning to eat. It's probably going to nail the squirrel now."

"I don't think that's a squirrel," suggested Daniel. "It's colored like a chipmunk."

"It's too big for a chipmunk, and besides, we don't have chipmunks here," said Dad

"We don't have eagles like that here either, Dad," added Daniel.

No one turned their heads away from what Dad thought was going to be the doom of the smaller animal. They were too fascinated with the unusual goings on to want to miss any of it, even if it turned out to be unpleasant. Then a strange thing happened. The squirrel—or very large chipmunk—picked up what the eagle dropped and disappeared back into the rocks. The eagle returned its gaze toward the rock fort.

"That was very strange," said Dad.

"That was more than strange," said Daniel. "That was bizarre."

"Now will you believe us?" asked Rebekah.

"Believe what?" asked Dad.

"Our dream, Daddy, it was real. That's Bomber," said Rebekah, nodding toward the eagle. "Daddy, that's one of the eagles in our dream… the one we saw at Christmas Bear's house."

Dad's eyes narrowed as he looked at Rebekah, but didn't say anything. They all stood there for several minutes just looking at the eagle. The eagle just kept looking back at them.

"Hey, look over there!" said Daniel—pointing to the trail leading from the back gate to the rock fort.

Everyone looked to see an animal scampering down the trail toward them. It would not have been an unusual sight, except that this animal was definitely a large chipmunk, and it was carrying something in its mouth.

"It's Zeek!" said Rebekah. "I can't believe this!"

The chipmunk stopped in the clearing just east of the rock fort and dropped what it was carrying on the ground. It stood there a moment and looked at the humans. It then let out a loud chatter and went back up the trail and disappeared into the brush.

Daniel jumped off the rock to go see what the chipmunk dropped. Rebekah and Jonas followed him. Daniel picked up the object and Rebekah and Jonas huddled around him.

Jonas yelled, "It's my cuff, it's my cuff!"

Rebekah jumped up and down in excitement and looked back to her dad, "It **is** Bomber, Daddy, and our dream was real! He and Zeek brought the cuff back from Treetop!"

Dad joined the group. Daniel put the torn cuff next to Jonas' torn sleeve. It matched Jonas' torn sleeve perfectly.

"Maybe the eagle just picked up your torn cuff off the ground," suggested Dad as he tried to make sense of these odd happenings. "Maybe the eagle…" Dad stopped that reasoning. *That wouldn't explain the chipmunk,* he thought. *An eagle and a chipmunk working together?*

"Daddy, smell," said Jonas as he held out his torn cuff to his dad. "It smells like pine!" said Jonas excitedly.

Sure enough, the cuff had a very distinct pine smell.

Just then, the eagle screeched again. The chipmunk reappeared on the ledge with the eagle, and to everyone's amazement, climbed onto the back of the great bird. The eagle stooped over and picked up something off the ledge with his beak. The eagle then jumped off the ledge and glided to the top of the big slide rock north of the sit-rock. He landed briefly, dropped what he was carrying on the rock and immediately took off again. The chipmunk lifted an arm toward them.

"Zeek's waving, Rebekah," said Jonas as both children waved back.

"Chipmunks don't wave!" said Dad.

"That one did," chuckled Daniel.

Dad glanced sideways at Daniel.

"Well, it looked like it waved," muttered Daniel shrugging his shoulders. "What's stranger, Dad, a chipmunk waving at you—or a chipmunk waving at you from the back of a flying eagle?"

"Ok, ok," said Dad, "I see your point."

They all stood by the slide rock and watched the eagle until he flew out of sight over the hill east of their property.

As soon as the eagle was out of sight, Rebekah and Jonas started running to the slide rock to see what the eagle had left there.

"You two wait by the slide rock until I get there," shouted Dad after them.

Rebekah and Jonas waited for Dad and Daniel at the base of the rock. When Dad arrived, he told everyone to stay where they were while he checked out what the eagle had left there. Dad climbed up the back of the slide rock, sat at the top, and picked something up.

When dad didn't say what it was right away, Rebekah asked, "What is it Daddy? What is it?"

Dad scooted down the slide rock to where Daniel, Rebekah, and Jonas were waiting and held up a tiny house for them to see.

"Oh, Daddy, let me see it closer! Let me see it closer!" said Rebekah excitedly

Dad slid off the rock and handed the little house to Rebekah. The house was snow white with a red roof and brown eaves. There was a big red front door with small Christmas trees on each side of it. There was a green wreath hanging on the red door. The windows on the sides of the house had red shutters with a holly design carved into them.

"It's the little house from Christmas Bear's tree!" exclaimed Jonas.

"It is, Daddy, it is!" said Rebekah confirming Jonas' observation. "It's from Christmas Bear's tree. It looks just like the little tree cottage we fell asleep in at the Summit." She turned to Jonas and handed him the little house. "It was real, Jonas, our dream was real!"

Jonas looked up at Dad with a big smile and said, "I didn't tear my jacket on the rock, Dad. The wolf tore it just like I said."

Dad was rubbing his chin trying to make sense of the eagle, the chipmunk, the cuff, and the little house. "I can't explain it," said Dad looking at Daniel. "Can you?"

Daniel shrugged his shoulders and said, "It makes no sense unless their dream is true."

"How can that be?" said Dad mostly to himself.

"It can be if God wants it to be," said Jonas confidently.

Dad and Daniel looked at Jonas and Rebekah. Jonas was smiling at them and Rebekah was shaking her head in agreement with Jonas.

"Ok, let's go down to the house. I want you to tell me your dream… or whatever it was…all over again. I want you to tell me every detail that you can remember. I'm going to take notes while it is fresh in your minds," said Dad.

They all walked back to the house. Dad went to his room to get a notebook. Daniel went to the stove and started the kettle heating. Rebekah and Jonas found Mom and Sarah in the school room and showed them Jonas' cuff and the little house. As the events of the morning up in the brush became known to the rest of the family, the questions started to fly. Dad announced that there would be a family gathering by the Christmas tree as soon as everyone had their tea, coffee, or hot cocoa. Soon everyone was sitting around the tree waiting for an explanation of the strange happenings Rebekah and Jonas had shared with them.

"As hard as I have tried," started Dad, "I can't explain what happened up in the brush, unless as Daniel said, Rebekah and Jonas' dream is real."

"How can that be?" asked John skeptically.

"Jonas," said Dad, "Tell John how that can be."

Jonas beamed as he said, "Like I told Dad, it can be true if God wants it to be."

John looked at Jonas, at Dad, and then just sat back with his arms crossed on the couch.

Dad continued, "I'm going to have Rebekah and Jonas tell us their story all over again, only this time I want everyone to listen very carefully and ask questions as they come to you. I'm going to take notes while this whole thing is fresh in their minds. These strange things haven't happened for no reason, since we all know that God has a reason for everything. "So," Dad turned to Rebekah and Jonas, "start from the very beginning and tell us again all about Treetop."

Rebekah and Jonas, both sitting cross-legged in front of the Christmas tree with their cocoa and with the little house dangling from the tree behind them, loved having the attention of the whole family.

"Well," said Rebekah, "it all started when Jonas and I went up to the sit-rock this morning…."

**The end**

---

**Cedar Rest Boulder**

# Appendix A:

# A Jabekah and Ronas Story

There is a Jabekah and Ronas story mentioned in *Treetop* in chapters 4 and 12; that story was originally called "Christmas Bear." It was a story I told my kids about two puppies, Jabekah and Ronas, who were helped by Christmas Bear on Christmas Eve night. The puppies got lost in a forest doing mischief, and Christmas Bear helped them get back home. The "Christmas Bear" story was the basis for the development of *Treetop*.

The Jabekah and Ronas story in this appendix is one about the puppies getting into mischief again. This time Christmas Bear is not there to help them.

# One Distraction Too Many!

## By J. J. Dyer

# Table of Contents

# One Distraction Too Many!

## (A Jabekah & Ronas Story)

## Chapter 1:

# *Rule Breakers*

Once upon a time there were two little German Shephard puppies named Jabekah and Ronas. They lived in a perfect little house at the edge of a beautiful pine and aspen tree forest. They were very strong and healthy puppies because God had blessed them abundantly. They had a mom and dad who loved them very much, and they had older brothers and a sister that loved them, too. Jabekah and Ronas were very good puppies. Most of the time they did what they were told, but every once in a while they thought that obeying was not so much fun. Since they liked fun so much, and since they got distracted so easily by so many interesting things, sometimes they disobeyed. This is a story about one of those times.

It was a very crisp morning that Saturday. Jabekah and Ronas had just woken up. They were stretching and yawning and trying to blink the sleep out of their little eyes. They were relaxing in their beds and thinking about the yummy breakfast they were going to eat when Mom peeked into their room.

"I thought I heard you waking up in here," she said with her

good-morning smile. "I am going to fix you pancakes with strawberries for breakfast this morning. What do you think about that?"

Jabekah and Ronas yipped with glee and jumped around so much
that they knocked the covers right off their beds.

"Calm down," Mama said. "I'm going out to the garden to get the
strawberries. Get up, wash your face and brush your teeth. We'll eat as
soon as you get to the table."

Mama then disappeared down the hall on her way to the garden.

Jabekah and Ronas should have run down the hall to the bathroom
to wash their faces and brush their teeth, but they didn't. Instead, they
ran to the kitchen window to watch their Mama disappear through her
garden gate on her way to the strawberry patch.

"Boy oh boy! I can't wait to taste those strawberries!" barked Ronas.

Unfortunately, Jabekah's mind wasn't on strawberries just then. She
had spied a bird on the lawn and was watching it gather his breakfast.

"That bird is getting his breakfast from **our** property and he didn't
ask **me** for permission. I think I'm going to run him off. Want to run
him off with me, Ronas?"

Ronas' was also watching the bird now, and his tail began to wag a
little as he thought of him and Jabekah giving that bird a scare.

"Maybe we should ask Mom if we can chase it before we go outside,"
suggested Ronas, remembering that they weren't supposed to go out
the backdoor unless they asked for permission first.

"Ok, we won't chase it. Let's just go out on the porch and let him
know that we are watching him."

After some discussion about whether or not they should go out on
the porch, they decided it wouldn't hurt anything if they just went out
on the porch for a few minutes to show the bird he wasn't getting away
with anything they weren't allowing to happen. So Jabekah and Ronas
snuck quietly out the back door, stuck out their tiny little chests, and
glared at the bird for daring to eat breakfast off their grass without their
permission.

There they were, standing on their porch, trying to look as tough as two little puppies could, but the bird paid them no mind. He just kept on eating his breakfast. What made matters even worse—he kept hunting for his food closer and closer to the porch!

Ronas was not too pleased with the bird's behavior. He had expected the bird to fly away as soon as he and Jabekah got on the porch. Little birds were supposed to run away from German Shephard puppies. It was a rule, and that bird wasn't following the rule.

"Maybe we should walk down the porch stairs and stand in the grass. Maybe that bird can't see so good. Maybe that's why he isn't flying away like he should. We should get a little closer so he can take a good look at who's watching him!" said Ronas indignantly.

Jabekah wasn't so sure. She knew she wasn't even supposed to be outside on the porch. Going down on the grass was being a little more disobedient than she felt comfortable with, but then the bird hopped even closer to Jabekah and Ronas. That final act of defiance was too much for Ronas to take. Ronas bolted off the porch toward the bird. Jabekah, startled by Ronas' quick departure, immediately followed after her determined brother without thinking another thought about staying on the porch. She'd seen her brother tear off like this before, and it usually meant he was headed for mischief. She figured she better run after him in case he ended up needing some help.

Ronas was doing his best to growl as he ran toward the bird. Jabekah began to giggle as she followed on Ronas' heels. Jabekah knew how to growl because she was a little older than Ronas, and whatever that sound Ronas was making—it wasn't a growl. Ronas heard the giggles, and that made him more determined to show that bird who was boss of his backyard.

When Ronas started his charge, the bird was about 100 puppy steps from the porch. There were about 75 puppy steps between Ronas and the bird when the bird turned to face Ronas, opened his sharp beak, and stretched out his wings—as if defying Ronas to come any closer. When Ronas was about 50 puppy steps from the bird, something much unexpected happened. Instead of flying away from Ronas, the bird started running at Ronas, flapping his wings and making an awful sound. After a dozen bird steps, the bird was airborne and flying right at Ronas' face.

Jabekah and Ronas hadn't had too much experience with birds. They knew what a bird looked like, but they couldn't tell one kind of bird from another. This particular bird was a mockingbird. And it just so happened that this particular mockingbird had quite a bit of experience with puppies—and they were all bad. Puppies routinely interrupted his breakfasts with their clumsy charges and pitiful growls.

"Don't these dumb dogs know they can't catch birds?" muttered the mockingbird to himself as he flew toward his attackers. This mockingbird was in no mood for a puppy encounter that morning, and he decided to let them know it.

When that mockingbird took off in Ronas' direction, Ronas immediately put on his puppy brakes. Jabekah hadn't seen the bird turn on them, so she kept running at full speed. Jabekah slammed right into Ronas' skidding backside. Both puppies tumbled head over heels toward the bird. The bird made a peck at Ronas as he swooped past the tumbling balls of fur and took a bit of puppy hair for his trouble. Ronas felt the bird take a chunk of his fur and he yelped in puppy outrage.

When the tumbling stopped, Jabekah and Ronas were sprawled on the grass. Both were soaking wet from rolling in the morning dew. Jabekah was looking at her and Ronas' wet fur. She began to wonder how they were going to explain the wet fur to Mama. After all, Mama had told them to wash their faces and brush their teeth before breakfast. Mom and Dad had told them not to go outside the house without asking first. And Jabekah was just beginning to recall Daddy saying something about leaving birds alone when she noticed the bird sitting on the gutter of the house staring at them. Right at that moment, the bird came at them again.

Jabekah was the only one to see the bird begin its dive toward them. Jabekah jumped up and began running for the cover of the forest that ringed their house. As she ran she shouted, "Ronas, run! He's coming back!"

Now Ronas hadn't taken his face out of the grass since their collision. When he did look up, all he saw was Jabekah's backend "high tailing" it to the pine trees. He heard her saying something, but he couldn't make it out because Jabekah was talking to the front of her and Ronas was way to the back of her. He'd seen his sister tear off like this before when she saw trouble coming, so he figured he better run now and find out what the trouble was later.

Ronas took off just as the mockingbird swooped to peck another patch of fur from Ronas' head. His quick, side-ways puppy-start threw off the aim of the mockingbird. Ronas ran after his sister into the Pine trees and the mockingbird soared up in the air—furless this time.

When Ronas reached the trees, he saw Jabekah sitting on top of a big rock looking into the sky.

"Why did you run over here?" asked Ronas, looking up at Jabekah and taking a seat to rest from his sprint. "You know Mom and Dad don't want us in the woods unless they are with us."

"Didn't you see that crazy bird attacking us again?" replied an out-of-breath Jabekah – not taking her eyes off the piece of sky that was visible through the trees. "He turned and came back at us from the house! There was nowhere else to go! Didn't you hear me tell you to run?"

Ronas turned and began searching that same piece of sky as he said, "How was I supposed to hear you yelling at the pine trees? How many times has Dad told you to speak directly at the person you're talking to so they can hear you?"

"Oh! I'm **so** sorry! Next time we're being attacked by some crazy bird, I'll run backwards so you can hear me better!"

Ronas was thinking about nipping his smart-mouthed sister's tail when he heard footsteps in the forest somewhere behind Jabekah. Jabekah had heard them, too. Both puppies jumped up, turned, and froze—staring off in the brush at the foot of the trees to see what was making the noise.

As the puppies completed their turn, the footsteps abruptly stopped. Jabekah and Ronas gave their full attention to the brush right in front of them. Their little puppy minds were now completely filled with a mixture of fear and excitement over the source of these mysterious footsteps.

Jabekah and Ronas kept very still. They had watched their Daddy do this many times when he wanted to see what type of critter was making noises in the brush. Dad would remain still until the noise started up again, and then he would go see what was there. But puppies aren't Daddies. And Daddy wasn't with them. And the longer Jabekah and Ronas waited to hear the footsteps again, the more they both began to think that maybe they might not want to meet up with whatever was making those footsteps.

"Jabekah," whispered Ronas, "do you think those were big footsteps or little footsteps?"

"I don't know," whispered Jabekah. "They stopped too quickly for me to make a guess."

"Well," said Ronas in a somewhat worried whisper, "if we don't know if they were big footsteps or little footsteps, why are we waiting around here to find out?"

Jabekah was thinking about the wisdom of Ronas' question when the footsteps started up again. Both puppies jumped back at the sound. Jabekah almost fell off the rock she was on. They were just about ready to run back to their house when a gray squirrel broke from the brush and began running away into the forest.

This was not a good decision-making morning for Jabekah and Ronas. First of all, at that very moment, they should have been in their bathroom finishing their face washing and teeth brushing. But they weren't. They had gone to the window to watch their mother go into the garden instead of going directly to the bathroom. At the time, that seemed to be no big deal. But once they looked out the window, Jabekah had seen that crazy bird. With their puppy minds filled with thoughts of scaring off that bird, they forgot all about Mama in the garden and their bathroom duties. Once they were on the porch, one distraction led to another distraction bringing them to where they were now—in the forest watching a squirrel run off deeper into the forest. Jabekah and Ronas, with their puppy minds now filled with squirrel thoughts, were about to make their biggest mistake of the morning.

"She's getting away!" shouted Ronas, and he was off like a shot after that squirrel.

*Getting away?* Thought Jabekah. We *never had her. How can she be getting away?*

Those few thoughts only took a few seconds, but it only took those few seconds for Jabekah to begin losing sight of Ronas. All she could see was Ronas weaving around pine trees that got in his way as he tried to keep the squirrel in sight. Ronas was doing his fastest puppy run, but he still wasn't too good at running in a straight line. A good thing, too, because if he had been running in a straight line, it might have been harder to see where he was going.

Without using up any more seconds to think, Jabekah began chasing after Ronas so she wouldn't lose him in the trees. Once she started running, most of her puppy thoughts went to catching glimpses between the trees of Ronas' wildly wagging tail. The rest of her puppy thoughts went to wondering what puppies were supposed to do with a squirrel if they caught one.

And Jabekah and Ronas chased that squirrel deeper…and deeper… and deeper into the forest.

As Jabekah and Ronas ran deeper and deeper into the forest, Mama was returning from gathering her strawberries and was getting closer and closer to the house. She noticed the backdoor was ajar, and shook her head thinking she hadn't closed it properly on her way out.

*I wonder if any critters got into the house when I was in the garden?* She said to herself as she closed the door and put the strawberries in the sink to wash them off.

Of course, we know a better question would have been, "I wonder what critters got OUT of the house when I was in the garden?" But how would Mama know to ask that question? She thought her puppies were in the bathroom doing what they were told to do.

After a few minutes into the chase, the gray squirrel knew she was dealing with a couple of amateurs. She loved to be chased by dogs for the exercise, and these dogs were not giving her much of that. These dogs were slow! She had to slow down a number of times to keep the chase going. Once she even doubled back and chased them for a while. They didn't even know she was behind them until she raced past them on the path. It was when she passed them that she realized she was being chased by a couple of puppies.

The gray squirrel knew that puppies didn't think too much before starting a chase. She also knew that puppies could easily get lost in a forest. Since she was a very considerate squirrel, she decided to end her exercise session, but not before having a little more fun first.

Ronas was getting tired. He tried his best to keep up with the squirrel, but he just couldn't seem to gain any ground on her. Once he was right on her tail, and he thought he was about to win this chase. At that moment, the squirrel glanced back, gave him what looked to him to be a squirrel smirk, and took off like a bullet. Soon the squirrel was so far ahead that he could hardly see her anymore. Ronas was getting discouraged.

Jabekah was getting angry. She was having a hard time catching up to Ronas because of his head start and because of all the brush and logs the squirrel had passed through or run over. On top of that, Jabekah knew that she was farther in the forest than she had ever been before, and she didn't like the fact that she was going farther and farther in trying to catch up with that brother of hers. Jabekah was beginning to get scared.

Just as Ronas was getting tired and discouraged…and just as Jabekah was getting angry and scared…and just as Jabekah had finally come up alongside her brother, they heard a rustling sound behind them. Before they could think much about that noise, their squirrel came from behind and ran past right between them! And before they could decide what to do about that embarrassing situation, the squirrel sped up and disappeared behind a tree about 25 puppy strides ahead of them. When they rounded that tree, they saw the squirrel again…still about 25 puppy strides ahead of them. But this time something was terribly wrong.

The gray squirrel was running right at Jabekah and Ronas!

Ronas was thinking, *Squirrels are not supposed to chase dogs! It was the rule, and that squirrel wasn't following the rule.* Ronas didn't have time to think another thought. Ronas jammed on his puppy brakes, skidded toward the advancing squirrel, and closed his eyes when the squirrel was just a few puppy feet away because he didn't know what else to do.

Jabekah was thinking, *Crazy birds and now crazy squirrels! God is punishing us for our disobedience.* Jabekah didn't have time to think another thought. Jabekah jammed on her puppy brakes, skidded toward the advancing squirrel, and closed her eyes when the squirrel was just a few puppy feet away because she didn't know what else to do.

Just as Jabekah and Ronas closed their eyes, the squirrel leaped over the puppies and onto the pine tree trunk behind them. She climbed to the first branch and looked down just in time to see the puppies skid into each other. She heard two yelps—more from fright than from pain—watched the ball of puppies tumble down the path and come to rest just before a huge boulder.

**Against The Rules**

## Chapter 2:

# Big Trouble

After Mama had rinsed the strawberries, she poked her head in the hall and yelled toward the bathroom, "Jabekah. Ronas. Hurry up. I need some help."

Mama then walked to the pantry and got out the things to make the pancakes. She took a bowl from under the counter and poured in the batter ingredients.

"If you want to help mix the batter, you better get out here," Mama said in a musical mama tone.

As Mama was getting some water for the batter, it dawned on her how quiet the house was. Normally, when Jabekah and Ronas are cleaning up for breakfast, you can hear them. As a matter of fact, when Jabekah and Ronas do anything together you can't help but hear them.

Mama put the water next to the batter bowl and headed down the hall toward the bathroom.

"Jabekah and Ronas. You better be in the bathroom getting cleaned up!"

Jabekah opened her eyes first. She found herself tangled up with Ronas' at the foot of a huge boulder. Ronas couldn't open his eyes yet because his face was buried in leaves and pine needles on the forest floor. The needles were poking his face and he dared not open his eyes for fear of getting them poked by the needles.

"Gefmmmmphmmmepf!" muffled Ronas.

Jabekah heard Ronas try to say something, but she couldn't understand what he said because his face was buried in leaves and needles.

"What did you say, Ronas?" Jabekah asked—still a bit shaken by their tumble.

"Gemmmmmophmmmmmmeph!" replied Ronas. "Mmmmmoommmmmeph!!"

"I still can't understand yo...."

Before Jabekah could finish her sentence, Ronas made a forceful push to his right that knocked Jabekah off his back. He pulled his face out of the pine needles and for the next few seconds spit needles, leaves, and dirt out of his mouth.

"Yuk!" complained Jabekah, wrinkling her nose in disgust.

Still on his belly, all four legs sprawled out on the ground, Ronas looked at Jabekah and said, "I was telling you to get off me so I could breathe!"

"How was I supposed to know what you were saying? You were talking into the dirt. Remember, Dad told you to always speak directly to a person if you want them to hear you?"

Ronas shot back, "How was I supposed to 'speak to you directly' with my face in the dirt and you on top of me?"

"Oh! I'm **so** sorry! Next time we're being attacked by some crazy squirrel, I'll just let you handle the whole thing without my help, so there!" Jabekah said angrily.

The squirrel found the puppies' banter entertaining. She chuckled and shook her head in amusement as she disappeared in the upper branches of the tree.

Jabekah and Ronas heard squirrel chatter in the tree above them. They looked up just in time to see a bushy gray tail disappear into the pine. They didn't know that the squirrel had found them amusing, but the chuckle chatter served a good purpose in that it interrupted their argument.

Jabekah and Ronas looked a mess. Their fur had gotten wet from tumbling in the dewy grass after the mockingbird flew at them. Now, after tumbling on the forest floor because of the squirrel attack, they were covered in dirt, leaves, and pine needles.

Jabekah got up and tried to shake herself clean, but the dirt stuck to her fur and she looked no better for her efforts. Ronas was still on his tummy catching his breath. Besides, he didn't mind being dirty as much as Jabekah did.

"This sure has been a strange morning." said Jabekah. "First that bird gave us trouble, and then we meet up with a wacko squirrel." "What's next?"

At that moment, Ronas was wishing that pancakes and strawberries were next.

There was a few minutes of quiet as the puppies rested by the boulder. Both were thinking about what they should do next. Ronas was the first to break the silence.

"We're in big trouble," Ronas said slowly as he stared at the boulder in front of him.

Jabekah didn't have a response at that very moment.

"We're in **big** trouble," repeated Ronas. That's all he could think of to say.

"Saying 'We're in Big trouble' over and over isn't going to help us any" replied Jabekah—annoyed by the truth of those words. "We just have to come up with a reasonable explanation about how we got so dirty, that's all."

"That's all?" Ronas asked, in a tone of disbelief.

"Well, we'll have to explain why we went outside…and why we went into the forest…and…"

Ronas interrupted Jabekah mid-sentence, "Who are you going to explain all this to?"

After a puzzled pause, Jabekah snapped, "To Mama, of course. Who else?"

"Where's Mama?" asked Ronas, still staring at the boulder.

Jabekah started wondering if Ronas had hit his head on that boulder. "She's home! We just left her there a few minutes ago. What's wrong with you?"

"Where's home?" asked Ronas, staring at Jabekah this time, knowing very well she had no idea where "home" was.

"Home is….home." Jabekah stammered. "It's…it's over there… somewhere…"

Jabekah found herself pointing to a wall of pine and aspen trees. No matter where she looked, all she saw was a wall of trees. And all the walls of trees looked the same to her puppy eyes.

"We're in big trouble," agreed Jabekah.

———— ✳ ————

**A Chastening**

# Chapter 3:

# The Search Begins

When Mama found the bathroom empty and no signs of two puppies cleaning themselves up, she went to their bedroom. No puppies there, either. Their beds were still unmade. No puppies in the garage. No puppies in their brothers' or sister's room. No puppies anywhere!

Mama went to her room to see if the puppies had woken up Dad. There was Dad's hulk stretched out on the bed. His paws were behind his head. He was looking at Mama when she came through the door.

"Are Jabekah and Ronas with you?" asked Mama rhetorically.

Dad didn't like rhetorical questions. He looked at the empty bed space next to him, lifted the covers for a peak, looked under his pillow, and said, "No."

"Well, where are they?" asked Mama, concern showing in her voice because her puppies were nowhere to be found. "Did they wake you up?"

"No. You woke me up." Dad said flatly.

"Honey, this is no time for you to be your normal 'helpful self.'" Mama said half-jokingly, but very seriously.

"The puppies are missing, and I don't know where they have gone!

It seemed like a long time before either of them spoke again, but it was actually only a few moments.

Jabekah broke the silence this time. "We can't be too far from home. We just left there a few minutes ago. How far could we have gotten in that little bit of time?"

Ronas didn't say anything. He hadn't moved and was still staring at the boulder. Jabekah was really beginning to wonder about him. After a few minutes, Jabekah broke the silence again.

"I think we should try to find our trail and follow it back to the house; that's what we should do. Come on Ronas, help me find our trail."

Ronas slowly sat up and turned his head to look at Jabekah. "What does a trail look like, and how do we follow it?"

Jabekah thought for a minute and then replied, "Paw prints! All we have to do is find our paw prints and follow them back home. What could be so hard about that?"

Ronas didn't reply right away. He was looking at the ground. All he saw in front of him were pine needles and aspen leaves. He looked all around and the ground everywhere was covered with pine needles and aspen leaves.

Jabekah was watching Ronas and followed his gaze to the ground surrounding them. Then it hit her...

"There are no paw prints in pine needles and aspen leaves," she moaned as she flopped down and lowered her head in despair.

During this silent period, Ronas got up slowly and walked around the perimeter of "their" section of the forest. When he finished, he came over and sat in front of Jabekah.

"It all looks the same. No tracks anywhere; just needles and leaves. We could just start back in that direction," motioning with his head in the direction of where he thought they had come. "It's better than just sitting here and doing nothing."

Jabekah looked around at all the trees and slowly said, "Noooo — that might be the wrong way. All the trees look alike...all the paths look alike...everything looks alike!" she blurted out in frustration.

"Well, I figure the longer we're gone, the more trouble we're going to be in! And besides, I'm getting hungry! I think we should try to find our way back."

"I remember Dad told us once that if we were ever lost, especially if we got lost in the forest, we were supposed to stay put until somebody found us. Don't you remember something like that?"

Ronas shook his head to get rid of a bothersome pine needle…and to shake his memory a bit. He did remember Dad saying something about staying put when you were lost, but he didn't want to remember the "forest" part because he didn't want to wait around to be found. He wanted to go home and eat!

"I'm not sure we're supposed to wait to be found in the forest," said Ronas. "If we wait here, we might be found alright—we might be found by a bear or a mountain lion!"

As soon as he said it, he wished he hadn't. Until then, neither he nor Jabekah had been thinking about bears or mountain lions. But once the thought was out, there was no taking it back.

Both Jabekah and Ronas were quiet for a while. After all, you can't listen for bears and lions very well while you're talking. And on top of that, bears and lions have good ears. They didn't want to give away their position with unnecessary chatter. Now all Jabekah and Ronas could think about were bears and mountain lions.

Jabekah's puppy mind was so full of bears and mountain lions that she didn't have any more room for her thought of Dad telling them to stay put when lost in the forest. Now she wanted to get moving—and moving fast…to anywhere but there.

"Let's try the way you suggested," whispered Jabekah. "That way," she motioned with her nose. "It's better than just sitting here waiting to be somebody's breakfast."

"Breakfast," Ronas whimpered as he stood up to go. "If only we had obeyed Mama and just gone to the bathroom."

They both started out, side by side, toward what they thought was the direction of their house. They hadn't taken more than a half dozen puppy steps when they were stopped in their tracks by a voice they had never heard before…

"You two better stop right there if you know what's good for you!"

Dad had gotten out of bed and muttered something about not being able to enjoy his morning coffee and Bible reading time. Mama had explained the events of the morning to him…as much as she knew them…and managed to convince Daddy that he needed to start looking for their wayward puppies.

"You said you found the door open when you came back with the strawberries?" Dad asked, trying to figure out where the puppies had gone.

"Yes, but I'm not sure if I closed it properly when I went out,"

Dad and mom stepped out on the porch. It was a beautiful, crisp morning. Dad was beginning to grumble again about his coffee and Bible time being messed up when he noticed the grass. The grass was covered with a very heavy dew because of the moist, almost freezing night. All of the grass was covered with this heavy dew except a small portion grass near the edge of the forest.

Dad stepped off the porch and walked toward the grass with no dew. He began grumbling about the cold, wet grass on his feet as he approached the area. He looked closely at the grass where the dew had been seemingly wiped away.

"Something has been rolling around in the grass," mentioned Dad emotionlessly.

"What do you mean, 'something' has been rolling around in the grass?" ask Mama, a mixture of fear and frustration showing in her voice.

"Something has been rolling around in the grass!" Dad repeated, as if saying the same thing again was supposed to give Mama additional information.

"Are you saying it looks like Jabekah and Ronas had been rolling around in the grass?" Mama asked, trying her best to be patient with her "overly expressive" husband.

"It probably was them," said Dad. "What were they doing out here?"

"They weren't supposed to be out here! If it was them, they were being disobedient! OOH, those two! What were they thinking?"

"They probably weren't thinking. It looks like they headed off into the forest about here," nodded Dad, following the trail of dewless grass to the edge of the woods. "Wake up Rahrah and tell her to watch for them at the house in case they come back on their own. If they should show up, have her send one of the boys after me. I'll see if I can pick up their trail. You can look around the property in case they're hiding around here." And with that, Dad disappeared in the woods.

---

**Don't Tempt Me!**

# Chapter 4:

# Foe or Friend

J abekah and Ronas were afraid to move. *Who had said that? Who was watching them? A mountain lion? A bear?*

Jabekah was the first to say anything. "Did you hear that?" she whispered, "Did that sound like a bear to you?" she asked fearfully.

"I think it was a lion," whispered Ronas. "I don't think bears talk much and their voices are probably lower."

"Do you think we should make a run for it?"

"Run for it where?" asked Ronas. "Do you know where to run? I couldn't tell where that voice was coming from."

"Are we just supposed to stand here like a couple of fools until we get ate?" whispered Jabekah desperately.

"Would you like to start running just any old place and end up running right into the lion's big mouth?" replied Ronas, the stress of the situation starting to show in Ronas' tone.

"Quit talking so loud," scolded Jabekah, more loudly than she had intended. "Do you want the lion to know what our plans are?"

"OOOOH, Pleeease Stop!" pleaded that same strange voice. "If I was a bear or a lion, you'd be food already!"

The voice was coming from above them. Both puppies slowly raised their eyes to the sky to see if they could see who was spying on them. Neither of them saw anyone.

"Jabekah," Ronas said in astonishment, "I didn't think trees could talk."

"They can't talk, silly! Trees can't talk! At least, they're not supposed to be able to talk. I've never heard one talk before and we've done a lot of business around a lot of trees. If they could talk, you'd think they would have said something to us by now. After all..."

"Stop it! Stop it! Stop it!" shouted the strange voice. "Why I've never heard such foolish chatter in all my days, and my head hurts from listening to it. Look up over here."

Both puppies looked toward the strange voice and saw a big gray squirrel sitting at the end of a pine branch.

"That's that wacko squirrel..." started Jabekah, but the squirrel cut her off.

"That's enough of that young lady!" snapped the squirrel. "I have heard just about all I want to hear about 'that crazy squirrel' and 'that wacko squirrel.' I won't help you if you keep on with your name-calling. If you can't keep a civil tongue, I'll just be on my way. Understand?"

The squirrel took their lack of response as an affirmative, so she continued.

"I couldn't help but overhear your conversation about being lost and all that. I wasn't being sneaky, mind you. I was just catching my breath up here like you were catching yours down there. Anyway, it sounds to me like you puppies have gotten yourselves in quite a fix. Tell me if I have everything straight."

"First, you disobeyed your Mama about going 'outside.' I assume that means you were told to stay inside, correct?"

The puppies didn't say anything, but the squirrel counted that as a blessing and continued.

"Then you disobeyed again by going into the forest. Why did you go into the forest when you weren't supposed to?" inquired the squirrel.

There was a long pause, and Jabekah sensed that the squirrel was waiting for an answer, so she began, "Well we were chasing this crazy bird and....."

"Stop right there, young lady!" snapped the squirrel. "Crazy, wacko squirrels! Crazy Birds! I don't see any squirrels or birds in trouble around here, do you? Seems to me a few puppies I know might think to examine their own mental state before they go about judging anyone else's. I do believe that's what our Creator has instructed us to do, isn't it?"

Jabekah and Ronas did remember Mama and Daddy telling them to be careful about making judgments about others. They also remembered Mama saying it wasn't nice to call others names; that was usually after Daddy had called someone a name though, so they were a little confused about that advice.

"Isn't it?!" The squirrel interrupted their thoughts with her demand for a reply.

"Yes, ma'am," they said softly in unison.

"Well, that's much better. Much better!" said the squirrel, sensing a change of attitude in both puppies.

"Now, what are we to do about your predicament?" said the squirrel.

"Our what?" asked Jabekah and Ronas simultaneously.

"Your situation…the mess you're in…your predicament," said the squirrel.

"If you could help us find our way home, that would fix our 'predickerment'" replied Ronas.

"That's 'predicament,'" corrected the squirrel.

"Whatever you call it," replied Ronas, "Helping us get home would fix it."

"Well, I could try to help you find your way," said the squirrel, "but there are quite a few houses scattered in this forest you know."

"We could describe our house to you to see if you know where ours is," suggested Jabekah.

"That might work, but I was thinking about something you were saying to each other just before you two got carried away with your lion and bear dialog." The squirrel waited to see if they remembered what they had said.

They didn't.

The squirrel gave them a hint, "Stay put if you get lost in the forest. Does that sound familiar?"

"That's what our Daddy says," offered Jabekah.

"Ah, and do you think that maybe, just maybe, you should do as he told you? I know how that would be contrary to everything else you have been doing all morning, but doing something contrary would be good in your case."

The squirrel's sarcasm was lost on the puppies, but they did get the idea that the squirrel was suggesting they should obey their dad and stay put.

They were just getting comfortable with the idea that they should just sit where they were until they were rescued, when they heard a crunch in the bushes off to their left. Jabekah, Ronas, and the squirrel stopped talking and started listening.

There was a long silence, and then the crunching started up again. It was a slow, deliberate crunching. It sounded like something heavy was out there somewhere. Something big. Something that wasn't trying to be very quiet. Something that didn't need to be quiet. Something like… like a lion or a bear.

The squirrel whispered quickly and quietly, "You puppies stay put and keep your mouths shut! I'm going to creep over the treetops to see if I can spot what's coming. Until I know what it is, we don't want to attract any more attention than we already have."

Ronas whispered back excitedly, "Don't leave us now! What if it's a lion?"

"Yeah," said Jabekah, "what if it's a bear! We may need some help here!"

"You two need help, alright, but not the kind I can give you." She shook her head and said, "Listen. What can I do for you here? Fight the bear or lion for you? Think, puppies, think! What **I can do** is find out what's coming. Knowing that, we can decide whether you should run or hide."

They all heard the heavy crunch again, except it was closer this time.

"Stay quiet and don't move!" whispered the squirrel and she was off.

The two puppies squatted as low as they could get on the ground next to the big boulder and stared in the direction of the noise. They had never been so scared in their entire lives.

**The Patriarch**

# Chapter 5:

# Bitter & Sweet

The gray squirrel was swift and quiet. She was seventeen trees from the puppies when she spotted a big hulk of a thing slowly coming in her direction. She couldn't see it clearly because it was partially blocked by the brush at the base of the trees. It was sniffing the ground, then looking up in the trees, and then looking in every direction around it. It was hunting…and it looked like it meant business. The squirrel was afraid she'd be noticed if she moved any closer, so she just stayed put and let the thing come to her.

As the hunter got closer to the squirrel, it looked more and more like a big wolf. The squirrel was fearing for the puppies when she caught a better glimpse of the creature. Its coloring was darker than most wolves. It didn't take long for her to realize that the "thing" she was watching was no wolf – but a very large German Shephard dog. He didn't look any friendlier than the wolves she'd seen, but since she knew dogs couldn't climb trees very well, she knew she was safe where she was.

The old dog looked like he could be related to the puppies—same coloring and all. When the huge dog was a few trees away, she sat up on the branch she was crouched upon. She knew the old dog had to have seen her, but he continued on his hunt without acknowledging her presence. Now she knew he wasn't friendly.

"Looking for something?" she asked, as the dog started moving away from her tree.

The old dog glanced up at the squirrel and said coolly, "I'm not looking for **you**."

The old dog didn't like squirrels much. Of course, most of his experience was with ground squirrels. They were filthy little rodents who dug holes everywhere and generally made a nuisance of themselves. He especially hated their speed and agility. They almost always won a chase. The old dog smiled to himself; the key word here was "almost." That meant that sometimes they didn't win.

His pleasant thoughts about ground squirrels losing chases were interrupted by the gray squirrel's question, "You wouldn't happen to be looking for two rambunctious puppies, would you?"

"Rambunctious," he thought. The old dog didn't like big words, and he didn't care for animals who tried to impress folks with them. However, the squirrel was still trying to be friendly even while he was trying not to be, and she obviously knew something about the puppies. Besides, she was a gray squirrel, not a ground squirrel. Gray squirrels were cleaner, bigger, more graceful, and lived in pine trees instead of holes in the ground. They were mountain squirrels—not coastal squirrels. He decided to be more sociable.

"I am looking for my two puppies, Jabekah and Ronas. They wandered off in the woods this morning without telling their mother. When did you last see them?"

"I just left them a few minutes ago by that huge rock over there," gesturing with her tail in the direction of the puppies. "They heard you coming through the brush. They think you are a lion or a bear. They have quite active imaginations, I've noticed."

"Yes they do," the old dog replied. "They take after their mother," he said with little emotion.

The squirrel didn't doubt it. She couldn't imagine this old dog having any imagination at all. "Would you like me to take you to them now?" the squirrel asked, trying to sound pleasant.

"No," said the old dog, "I'll find them alright myself….thanks for your help," he added, trying to sound grateful.

The old dog stood there for a long time, just staring in the direction where the puppies were hiding.

The squirrel scampered away in the treetops – thanking God she wasn't one of those puppies right now.

Jabekah and Ronas had watched the nice gray squirrel run off in the trees toward the crunching noise. Jabekah just knew it was a bear. Ronas was sure it was a mountain lion. They waited and waited for the gray squirrel to come back to tell them what they should do.

The wait seemed like forever to them, but the squirrel had only been gone for a few minutes. The sun began peaking over the trees behind the boulder Jabekah and Ronas were hiding by. The sun's rays lit up the shadowy morning forest in front of them. They were still in the shade of the boulder.

"This is great!" whispered Ronas. "We're still in the shadows and the whole place is lit up in front of us. We'll see the lion before it sees us. That will give us an advantage."

"An advantage to do what?" whispered Jabekah. "By the time we see him, he'll be right on top of us. Great advantage!" she said a little more loudly than she intended.

"Shush!" whispered Ronas. "He'll hear you! Remember, the squirrel told us to be quiet and still until she came back."

"Oh! The squirrel said! The squirrel said! We haven't listened to Mama and Daddy all morning and we're in big trouble because of it. Now some strange squirrel gives you advice and all of a sudden you're mister obedience! I just want to get out of here…now!" said Jabekah frantically and still a little too loudly.

They barely heard a noise just off to their right about 60 puppy steps away. They only "barely" heard the noise because they were making too much of their own arguing about their situation. They scooted back closer to the boulder. Everything was still and quiet; too quiet. They were almost too scared to even breathe. They both starred in the direction where they thought the noise had come from.

Ronas thought he saw something briefly flash in the brush where he was looking. He squinted to see if he could make something out. He couldn't.

"Jabekah," he whispered, "did you see something flash out there?"

Jabekah was looking at the same place Ronas had been looking. She didn't acknowledge his question.

"Jabekah? Did you see it?" Ronas asked again.

Ronas opened his mouth to ask her the same question a third time when Jabekah whispered, "Eyes…..its eyes, Ronas…big.angry.yellow. eyes."

Ronas' mouth remained open but no words would come out. He could now see the eyes. The sun had moved up higher in the sky over the trees behind them and had shed its beams on the brush with the eyes. The eyes were glowing in the sunlight.

"Bushes aren't supposed to have eyes," whispered Ronas.

"Bushed don't have eyes, Ronas," Jabekah said impatiently. "It's something **in** the bushes."

"Yellow eyes? What has big angry yellow eyes, Jabekah? Tell me, what?" questioned Ronas in a low raspy voice.

Jabekah did have an answer.

"You see? I knew it. Nothing else has yellow eyes. It's the bush. That bush has yellow eyes!"

"It does not!" said Jabekah insistently.

"Have you ever seen a bush's eyes?" asked Ronas.

Jabekah didn't answer.

"You see? I knew it. You've never seen a bush's eyes, so you don't know if they are yellow or not."

Ronas would have continued with his "bushes have eyes" theory if he could have. You see, Ronas figured that even though thinking that bushes had eyes was a scary thought, bushes can't move. So if the bush had yellow eyes, so what? He and Jabekah would just get away from the bush. It was imaginative thinking, but such ponderings soon came to an end.

The yellow eyes started to get up! As soon as they moved, Jabekah and Ronas scooted further back by the boulder and discovered that the boulder was wider than they thought it was. It was completely blocking their escape to the rear. It was too steep and tall for them to climb. They were trapped good this time, and there was nothing else for them to do but turn and fight the "eyes."

Ronas attempted to growl before he turned to face the yellow eyed thing…just to give it a try one last time. It was pitiful. He tried again, but it was more of a moan than a growl.

Jabekah knew she would have to do the growling for the both of them. Her growl wasn't fierce yet, but at least it was a growl.

They quickly decided that they would turn to face "yellow eyes" at the same time and try to growl at the same time. With a double growl, they hoped beyond hope to somehow scare their enemy away.

They turned and advanced together toward the bush—truly believing that this was the last thing they might ever do together. They had no idea what they were about to face, and it turned out to be a real nightmare.

When they turned, they saw it. The yellow-eyed beast was huge. He looked mean. He looked angry. He looked just like Daddy.

"Daddy?" Jabekah said timidly. "Is that you?" As soon as she said it, she wished she hadn't. Daddy never let a stupid question go, and that was a really stupid question.

"Do you know anybody else who looks like this?" asked Daddy sternly.

"No, Daddy. Nobody." Jabekah answered assuredly.

Ronas tried not to make the same mistake Jabekah had just made. "We thought you were a bear...or a mountain lion...or a bush with yellow eyes, Daddy." Ronas offered weakly.

Daddy looked at both of them and said, "It would have been better for you if I was a bear, or a mountain lion, or a bush with yellow eyes. You can run from all those things."

Daddy was not in a good mood, and this conversation was not going in a direction that Jabekah and Ronas liked. As they struggled to come up with something to say that might lighten up the situation a bit, they heard something coming up on them fast from the west. Some type of fast moving animal, it seemed. And almost immediately, everything changed. Mama! Beautiful, kind, understanding Mama had arrived!

Mama bounded into the middle of the encounter with grace and beauty. She had white hair and a big bushy silver/white tail. Daddy had always admired Mama's silver/white tail. Even in his worst moods, she seemed to take the edge off him a bit. And Daddy needed an edging quickly.

"Jabekah! Ronas! You two put a fright into me this morning!" Mama was trying to look stern, but she was too happy to see Jabekah and Ronas to keep it up for too long.

"I'm so grateful you are safe and unhurt." Then she realized she hadn't asked them, "You're not hurt, are you?"

"No Mama, not yet," said Jabekah sadly, looking at Daddy.

Mama then went over to Daddy and said in a low, soothing voice, "Honey, please don't be too harsh with the puppies. After all, they are only puppies. Look at them, dear, they are dirty and scared. I know they must be disciplined for disobeying us. I know you can be firm and still be gentle. Try not to stay angry with them too long."

Daddy was looking at the puppies. They were scared alright, scared of what he was going to do to them for their disobedience. And they were very dirty, but only because they disobeyed in the first place.

"Puppies have to stop acting like puppies someday," answered Daddy. "This is a good time for it to stop. This 'puppy' excuse is getting old."

Uh oh. Daddy wasn't having any of it. *Don't stop now, Mama,* Jabekah thought, *Daddy's edge is still too sharp.*

"Well, Dear, I know you will do the right thing." replied Mama as sweetly as only Mama could.

Daddy's glare came off of us for just a second as he gave a sideways glance at Mama. He knew exactly what Mama was up to, and he always resisted her pleas for mercy on us, but her gentleness always worked its way through his hard bark a little. You could see it in his eyes—they were changing from cold and emotionless to just cold. That was a good sign believe it or not.

"Well, puppies," said Mama cheerfully, "I'm sure you and your Daddy have some things to settle. I'm going back to the house and have Rahrah start the pancakes. By the time you get home, they should be ready."

"Honey," she said sooo sweetly, "I'll have your coffee and your Bible ready for you."

Then, looking around at everyone with a bright smile on her face, she said, "Oh, Lord, I am so grateful for my puppies being found safe." And with that, she was off as quickly as she had come—bounding gracefully toward home.

Daddy was watching Mama as she disappeared into the trees. His eyes were changing from cold to just stern. Things were looking a little better for Jabekah and Ronas.

When Mama left, the spirit of joy and peace she brought with her diminished slightly, but only slightly! What a godly Mama they had! Both Jabekah and Ronas were in the middle of thanking God profusely for their mother and her effect on their father—-when Daddy spoke.

"You two are going to get a tail-nipping when we get home," he said sternly, but the anger and fierceness was gone from his face. "You scared your mother half to death, and you made me angry with your disobedience. There are snakes and lions and bears who would just love to catch little puppies like you alone in the forest. I told you that many times. I told you never to go outside the house without asking, and I told you never to go into the forest without your Mama or me with you. You must learn to obey. You must learn to think before you act. You must learn that there are unpleasant consequences for the bad choices you make. You can learn the easy way or you can learn the hard way…but you **will** learn. ”

“Yes, Daddy,” replied Jabekah and Ronas, in very trembly voices. They were losing some of the joy and peace that had come with their mother as they thought about the words of their father.

“And I don’t want any fussing about your punishment. You did wrong, and you will face up to it without complaint,” said Daddy, even more sternly.

“Yes, Daddy”, replied Jabekah and Ronas, sadly—but not as trembly as the last time.

“Do you want your nipping before or after breakfast?” Daddy asked.

What a choice! They had made a lot of choices that morning, and the choices they made were not so good. Jabekah and Ronas looked at each other, but didn’t exchange a word. After a few moments, Ronas spoke.

“We’ll do it however you decide,” choked out Ronas, in as manly a tone as a puppy could muster.

“We’ll do it before breakfast, then. We’ll get it over with, and you’ll be better able to enjoy your strawberries and pancakes.

Daddy looked at them a few more seconds and began to turn toward home. “Head ‘em up—move ‘em out.”

Daddy always said, “Head ‘em up—move ‘em out” when he wanted all of us to go someplace together. We never understood what the words meant exactly, or where he got the saying, but he only said it when he was in a decent mood. It was good to hear.

**The Matriarch**

# Chapter 6:

# One Way or the Other

The grey squirrel had rushed back to the trees above the puppies right after she had spoken to the old dog. She wanted to see how all this was going to work out. She had settled in a tree that she had anticipated would be exactly between the puppies and the old dog. She had arrived just as the puppies began to converse. She had expected that the puppies wouldn't be able to keep quiet for too long, and she was right. She shook her head in amusement as they progressed from talking about the benefits of the sunlight—to arguing about talking about the benefits of the sunlight—to an argument about whether they should stay put or run—to, finally, "bushes with eyes." She wondered why God had made dogs so inclined to impulsive behavior and strange thinking—if you could call their 'thinking' thinking. She wondered if God had created them just for squirrel exercise and entertainment; after all, she had thanked Him that day for both.

It was amazing how that old dog had gone from noisily crunching bushes to silently stalking his puppies to a distance where he could both hear and see them. She didn't know a big old dog could move so quietly, and she filed that away in her mind for future reference.

It was curious how the old dog just crouched there and watched his two puppies talk themselves into a lather. He just let their imaginations run wild, and then scared them silly with his well-timed appearance.

She really hadn't seen a pleasant outcome for this at all until the mother showed up.

What a beautiful influence she was on all of them; reassuring and loving to her puppies—encouraging and respectful of her husband. She lessened the tensions of an unpleasant situation without taking away from the seriousness of the issues to be addressed. And after doing all this in a matter of a few minutes, she exited by planting thoughts of the comforting home that awaited their return from their unfinished business. Beautiful motherhood!

The squirrel had been delighted as she watched God's assigned family roles play themselves out in the drama below her. She thought of her own husband and family, and how the Mom and Dad roles worked themselves out in very similar ways. "Yep," she said to herself, "God's plan is best!"

The gray squirrel watched as the old dog led his scraggly puppies—their ears down and their tails between their little legs—off into the trees towards home.

The squirrel scampered home to give her husband and squirreletts an extra hug or two. She was feeling especially appreciative of her family and wanted to get home before the feeling faded in the routines of the day.

You could hear Jabekah and Ronas quietly crying in their room from their tail nipping. Daddy had told them they could come out of their room when they were finished fussing.

The house smelled of pancakes as Rahrah, Jabekah and Ronas' older sister, took them off the stove and placed them on a big platter.

John and Danda, Jabekah and Ronas' older brothers, were trying to calm the little puppies so they all could eat their breakfast.

Dad was sitting at the table, finally enjoying his cup of coffee and reading his Bible.

Mama stood back and took all this in. As you might have expected, she was grateful for the Lord's mercy and for the blessings He had poured on her family—and she was telling Him so at that very moment.

"Let's eat!" thundered Daddy.

Everyone headed for the table. Everyone was grateful that the morning had turned in a more positive direction. Even Daddy was grateful—in his daddy sort of way.

As Jabekah and Ronas passed the window to take their seats, Ronas looked out—and saw the bird back on the lawn. He nudged Jabekah and whispered, "Jabekah, that crazy bird is stealing food from our lawn again."

Jabekah looked out the window and frowned at the bird. "We'll take care of him after breakfast!" she whispered back.

Jabekah & Ronas turned to the table to find Daddy frowning at them.

"Leave-the-birds-alone!" Daddy said slowly with a bit of bite in his voice.

"Yes, Daddy," replied Jabekah and Ronas in unison.

Daddy just looked at the both of them.

"Here's the pancakes and strawberries!" said Mama cheerfully, as she and Rahrah brought the breakfast to the table. "Jabekah, why don't you thank God for our breakfast this morning?"

Everyone bowed their heads to pray.

"Thank you, God, for this nice day…for it turning out to be a nice day. Thank you for our family and for these good strawberries and pancakes. Thank you for protecting Ronas and I when we were in the forest—even though we weren't supposed to be in the forest. Thank you for the squirrel who tried to help us, and for Mommy and Daddy finding us so fast." Jabekah took a quick glance out the window. "And thanks for providing breakfast for birds, too. We thank you in Jesus' name."

"That was a thoughtful prayer, Jabekah!" said Mama.

"It was a good prayer." said Daddy.

Jabekah smiled as she looked out the window.

"Leave the birds alone," reminded Daddy, this time only looking at his pancakes.

Jabekah and Ronas were thankful for being home. God had worked everything out for them without serious consequences this time. They prayed that they would learn His lessons the easy way – by recognizing, listening to, and obeying wise instruction. The hard way was not pleasant, and as their Daddy said, they will learn one way or the other.

The pancakes and strawberries tasted exceptionally good to them that morning.

---

**There'll Be Days Like This**

# Appendix B:

# Chapter Verses for Discussion – Treetop & One Distraction Too Many

If you read *Treetop* to others, I offer these verses as a help to start discussions about the situations in each chapter.

**Chapter 1: Psalms 34:7**
The angel of the LORD encamps around those who fear Him, and He delivers them.

**Chapter 2: Isaiah 26:3**
You will keep in perfect peace him whose mind is steadfast because he trusts in you.

**Chapter 3: Hebrews 13:2**
Do not forget to entertain strangers, for by so doing some people have entertained angels without knowing it.

**Chapter 4: Ephesians 4:29**
Do not let any unwholesome talk come out of your mouths, but only what is helpful for building others up according to their needs, that it may benefit those who listen.

**Chapter 5: Philippians 4:13**
I can do everything through him who gives me strength.

**Chapter 6: Proverbs 12:18**
Reckless words pierce like a sword, but the tongue of the wise brings healing.

**Chapter 7: Proverbs 21:30**
There is no wisdom, no insight, no plan that can succeed against the LORD.

**Chapter 8: Psalms 139:2**
You know when I sit and when I rise; you perceive my thoughts from afar.

**Chapter 9: Proverbs 18:4**
The words of a man's mouth are deep waters, but the fountain of wisdom is a bubbling brook.

**Chapter 10: Proverbs 19:20**
Listen to advice and accept instruction, and in the end you will be wise.

**Chapter 11: Proverbs 3:5-6**
Trust in the Lord with all your heart and lean not on you own understanding; in all your ways acknowledge him, and he will direct your paths.

**Chapter 12: Psalms 37:7**
Be still before the LORD and wait patiently for him; do not fret when men succeed in their ways, when they carry out their wicked schemes.

**Chapter 13: 2 Corinthians 5:10**
For we must all appear before the judgment seat of Christ, that each one may receive what is due him for the things done in the body, whether good or bad.

**Chapter 14: Psalms 119:160**
All your words are true; all your laws are eternal.

**Chapter 15: Proverbs 10:19**
When words are many, sin is not absent, but he who holds his tongue is wise.

**Chapter 16: Proverbs 3:24**
When you lie down, you will not be afraid; your sleep will be sweet.

**Chapter 17: Proverbs 20:18**
Make plans by seeking advice; if you wage war, obtain guidance.

**Chapter 18: Deuteronomy 31:6**
Be strong and courageous. Do not be afraid or terrified because of them, for the LORD your God goes with you; he will never leave you nor forsake you.

**Chapter 19: Colossians 3:23**
Whatever you do, work at it with all your heart, as working for the Lord, not for men, since you know that you will receive an inheritance from the Lord as a reward. It is the Lord Christ you are serving.

**Chapter 20: Psalms 64:5**
They encourage each other in evil plans, they talk about hiding their snares; they say, "Who will see them?"

**Chapter 21: Romans 1:18**
The wrath of God is being revealed from heaven against all the godlessness and wickedness of men who suppress the truth by their wickedness.

**Chapter 22: Joshua 1:9**
Have I not commanded you? Be strong and courageous. Do not be terrified; do not be discouraged, for the LORD your God will be with you wherever you go.

**Chapter 23: Psalms 7:14-16**
He who is pregnant with evil and conceives trouble gives birth to disillusionment. He who digs a whole and scoops it out falls into the pit he has made. The trouble he causes recoils on himself; his violence comes down on his own head.

**Chapter 24: Proverbs 19:3**
A man's own folly ruins his life, yet his heart rages against the LORD.

**Chapter 25: Psalms 18:16**
He reached down from on high and took hold of me; he drew me out of deep waters.

**Chapter 26: Psalms 115:3**
Our God is in heaven; he does whatever pleases him.

## One Distraction too Many!

**Chapter 1: Exodus 20:12**
Honor your father and mother, so that you may live long in the land the LORD your God is giving you.

## Chapter 2: 2 Chronicles 16:9
For the eyes of the LORD range throughout the earth to strengthen those whose hearts are fully committed to Him.

## Chapter 3: Proverbs 14:15
A simple man believes anything, but a prudent man gives thought to his steps.

## Chapter 4: Proverbs 12:15
The way of a fool seems right to him, but a wise man listens to advice.

## Chapter 5: Proverbs 22:15
Folly is bound up in the heart of a child, but the rod of discipline will drive it far from him.

## Chapter 6: 1 Corinthians 10:13
No temptation has seized you except what is common to man. And God is faithful; he will not let you be tempted beyond what you can bear. But when you are tempted, he will also provide a way out so that you can stand up under it

**The Path Is Narrow**

# Appendix C:

# Original Cover Images of the Treetop Notebook Edition

I created this cover using a rubber stamp for the large pine trees in the center of the sketch. Then I drew in the details around the stamp to fill out the image.

**Treetop**

by J. "Daddy" Dyer

# Acknowledgements

I have been blessed with a devoted wife and five remarkable children. Without their civilizing influence, I doubt I would have written any stories. I am grateful for their impact on my life.

# *About the author*

My storytelling days began when I started telling bedtime stories to my kids. One of the stories I told them was about Jabekah & Ronas—two German Shephard puppies whose antics repeatedly got them into trouble. Since the original Jabekah & Ronas story is mentioned by some characters in *Treetop*, I wanted to share another Jabekah & Ronas story with you. It is in Appendix A and titled *One Distraction too Many!*

My faith deeply inspires my writing. I believe God's word and laws are often overlooked, misunderstood, and misapplied in life. The fear of the LORD is the beginning of wisdom and knowledge (Proverbs 1:7, 9:10). Exodus 20:20 further reveals that God tests us "...so the fear of the LORD will be with you to keep you from sinning." I hope my stories illustrate how embracing "the fear of the LORD" principle leads to trustworthy wisdom and knowledge—guiding us away from life's pitfalls and toward a deeper understanding of how to apply God's laws in all areas of life.

Now all has been heard; here is the conclusion of the matter: Fear God and keep his commandants, for this is the whole duty of man. For God will bring every deed into judgement, including every hidden thing, whether it is good or evil—Ecclesiastes 12:13-14

www.ingramcontent.com/pod-product-compliance
Lightning Source LLC
LaVergne TN
LVHW022036230525
811924LV00008B/226